Doctor Omega

Doctor Omega

a classic tale of space and time by
Arnould Galopin

adapted and retold in English by
Jean-Marc & Randy Lofficier

collector's edition
illustrated by E. Bouard
and J.-M.Breton

A Black Coat Press Book

Acknowledgements: We are indebted to Terrance Dicks, Gil Formosa, Chris Achilleos, David McDonnell, and Marc Madouraud.

English adaptation Copyright © 2003 by Jean-Marc & Randy Lofficier.
Cover illustration by Rapeno.
Interior illustrations by E. Bouard and J.-M. Breton.
Frontispiece Copyright © 2003 by Gil Formosa.
Foreword Copyright © 2003 by Terrance Dicks.

Visit our website at www.blackcoatpress.com

DOCTOR OMEGA

A CLASSIC TALE OF SPACE AND TIME BY
ARNOULD GALOPIN
ADAPTED AND RETOLD BY
JEAN-MARC & RANDY LOFFICIER

Cover by Gil Formosa

Foreword

Clearly, we can never know *all* the adventures of that mysterious travelling Time Lord known as the Doctor.

How could we?

Since he could, in theory, leave the UNIT laboratory in the sixties, depart on an adventure lasting weeks, months, even years, and still return, TARDIS willing, ten minutes after his departure in time for morning coffee with the Brigadier, the possibilities are infinite.

Twenty-seven years of television and ten years of original *Doctor Who* novels have given some indication of the immense scope of the Doctor's adventures.

Possibly, just possibly, there is more.

Written in France in the 1900's, *Doctor Omega* is the narrative of one Denis Borel, a man of letters who receives an unexpected inheritance and retires to Normandy to enjoy a life of leisure.

He discovers he has a mysterious neighbour, an eccentric, reclusive scientist called Doctor Omega.

There is something strangely familiar about this Doctor.

He is described, seen by Borel in a kind of vision as *"a tall, elderly man, all dressed in black, with slick white hair pulled back, except for a rebellious lock on his forehead. He was smiling an all-knowing, mephistophelean smile... His eyes were of a penetrating blue; they never wavered..."*

Borel eventually makes Doctor Omega's acquaintance and discovers him to be an inventor, a scientific genius of amazing powers.

They strike up a kind of friendship, and Borel learns of Doctor Omega's current plans. He is synthesizing a new element, a kind of living metal. From it he intends to build a ship...

He tells Borel that *his own people*, from who he is *estranged*, use this metal to build ships. "*Very special ships. Ships unbound by the shackles of space and time.*"

The ship, a projectile shaped vehicle, is eventually built, though not until after many dangerous experiments.

The ship is christened the *Cosmos,* and Doctor Omega invites Borel to accompany him on her maiden voyage.

"Doctor, I'm ready to follow you anywhere! To the ends of the Earth if you will!" cries Borel.

"Oh, I think we'll go further than that," says Doctor Omega with a smile.

The *Cosmos* takes them to Mars, the Mars of several billion years ago, with a breathable atmosphere and an amazing assortment of monstrous inhabitants, including reptilian warriors...

Written in France in the 1900's by Arnould Galopin, the book was recently re-discovered by my old friend Jean-Marc Lofficier, a *Doctor Who* scholar almost as eccentric as Omega himself, as part of his research for an encyclopaedia devoted to French science fiction.

With the help of his wife, Randy, Jean-Marc has now translated, and somewhat modernized, his fellow countryman's long-forgotten work.

It's an amazing tale in its own right. Whether or not it forms a previously unknown part of a larger saga, you must judge for yourself.

Of course, it *could* all be coincidence...

Terrance Dicks

Chapter One
A Man of Mystery

The Narrative of Denis Borel, November 1905.

How did I meet Doctor Omega?

It is, as they say, a long story... A strange story... Amazing... Unimaginable, and perhaps it would have been better if I had never met him at all!

My life would not have been overturned by events so incredible that I sometimes ask myself if I have not dreamed the fantastic adventure I lived through, and which made me into a hero, even though I was at its onset the least daring of mortals.

But my own notebooks, my pictures, and the mementos of my journey are here, on my desk, to remind me that this was all too real.

No! I did not dream it... I was not the victim of some extravagant hallucination...

For approximately sixteen months, I actually visited another world.

What strange creature is man!

It is almost always when one has reached a state of serenity, when one finally enjoys the rewards of the happiness one has much longed for, that one cannot help but find new ways of tormenting oneself.

After seeking fortune for many years, without success, I had had the unexpected luck of inheriting a million francs from a half-forgotten uncle, whom I always thought was poor as a churchmouse because he lived in an old dilapidated shack, and wore clothes that literally hung together by only a few threads.

Yet, after his death, a thousand bank notes, each worth a thousand francs, had been found under his mattress–where else?

Yes, they were a bit rumpled, but I beg you to believe that they looked wonderful to me, and I had no difficulty in accepting them.

As soon as I had invested that proverbial windfall, I began looking for a suitable property in the countryside to which I could retire and enjoy a life of undisturbed leisure.

Near Marbeuf in Normandy, where I was born, I found an attractive cottage surrounded by five acres of woods and land. So, I happily left behind the all-too-turbulent Parisian scene which had consumed so much of my energy, and which had seen too many of my hopes wither and die.

Because of my newfound wealth, I, who had been a hard worker, a tireless man of letters, and an avid reader, decided to no longer write, or even read. I had almost nearly stopped reading altogether.

In spite of this, I did not find my new existence tiresome in the least.

It would seem that some natures do not have to have myriad things to keep them entertained or busy, and that which may seem boring to some, may in fact be a source of constant surprises and wonderful sensations to others.

Every type of outside activity, planned or otherwise, sounded like a discordant, even painful, cacophony to my sensitive ears.

My fondest wish was to hear one sound and one sound only, that of the music which I loved most: my violin's.

For I did not tell you that one thing, and one thing only, was still connecting me to the rest of society: an abiding passion for music.

I had purchased a genuine Stradivarius from the estate of a great musician who had suddenly passed away while playing one of Spohr's concertos, and thus I had been lucky to get my hands on this incredible instrument for far less than its real value: forty-five thousand francs.

That figure, I know, will bring a superior smile to the faces of all who hate music.

To spend forty-five thousand francs for a violin when, for the same amount, one could purchase a brand new fifty horsepower automobile! Madness, some will say!

Perhaps, but ultimately a matter of taste.

I much preferred playing the old masters on my Stradivarius than racing madly on the local roads at fifty miles an hour.

Thus, I spent all my time fiddling on my marvelous instrument with a bow made from genuine horse hair and Pernambouc wood, the construction of which was a pure artistic wonder.

As soon as I was up, I settled behind my stand and worked relentlessly on the rendering of a concerto by one of my favorite composers: Paganini, Alard or Vieuxtemps.

No one could say that I performed for the purpose of impressing my fellow human beings, for I played alone.

I was merely a solo violinist, filled with the art of music, passionate, tireless–and modest.

From time to time, I was visited by an old friend, a fellow from the Academy of Arts and Letters, with whom I had once collaborated on a few books that had gathered a modest success.

I must confess that when that friend rang the bell at the gate, and I saw his lanky silhouette walk towards my house in the park, I could not repress a gesture of irritation.

I did my best to be a pleasant host–one does not turn into a hermit so easily–but after a whole day of his company, I started to look forward to his leaving. The next day, I could but barely bring myself to pay attention to his words and, while he discussed the recent discovery of a medieval grimoir, I was in my head distractedly reviewing a Beethoven sonata.

Eventually, my friend must have found me as big a bore with my violin as Molière's *Monsieur Jourdain* was with his poetry, for he stopped coming, which suited me just fine.

Sometimes, my eyes tired of concentrating on chord diagrams, and my fingers lost their nimbleness from excessive use, leading to a marked deterioration of my playing.

Then, I carefully packed my instrument in its case, an authentic seventeenth century masterpiece, and went to sit for a while in a small gazebo located at the other end of my park, overlooking the main road.

There, while idly thinking about my next sonata, aria, or cantilene, I let my eyes wander about the surrounding countryside.

As far as they could see, there were woods amongst which one could perceive the occasional steeple or slated rooftop of a neighboring castle. Below me, in the valley, a few local houses crunched together next to a barely manageable street, just off the main road. They were all built according to the same trite and ordinary design: their walls made of red and black bricks, laid out symmetrically, making them look like giant chessboards.

At the other end of that which could only have been called a village by pretentious map-makers, there was a smaller hollow, with two larger buildings made of tarred wood, which I had always thought to be factories or warehouses of some kind, or possibly hangars for an aeroplane or a dirigible.

These two lugubrious buildings marred my otherwise perfect rural view, but I did not mind them too much...

Besides, when it came to matters of rural aesthetics, I had to confess an almost total lack of appreciation.

Thus, one evening, I was sitting in my gazebo, and my mind had become so absorbed by some new melody, that I had failed to notice that night had fallen...

I was about to get up and return to my house when, suddenly, before my eyes, a prodigious light leaped to the sky, spreading out like the wings of a giant dragon... Its brilliance illuminated the entire landscape, and a tremendous noise, like the deafening roar of a thousand waterfalls, filled the valley. The ground itself shook like in an earthquake.

I was thrown out of my rocking chair and fell to the ground, while the glass windows of my gazebo shattered around me, spreading me with a painful rain of shards.

I screamed.

My gardener and my manservant rushed to my assistance, and helped me back to my feet. They looked as shaken as I was, but whether it was because of the unexplained phenomenon, or because they may have been worried about losing an employer that paid them well and required comparatively little service in return, I could not guess. When they saw that I was unharmed, they regained their normal composure.

"What... What was that? What just happened?" I asked.

A neighbor who had rushed out of his house and was running towards the village on the road just below my gazebo heard my question, and shouted back at me:

"One of Doctor Omega's hangars just exploded!"

He continued running, obviously in a hurry to check on the welfare of his friends or family.

"Doctor Omega? Doctor Omega?" I muttered, looking at my servants. "Who is he? Do you know him?"

"He's an old eccentric who doesn't talk to anyone from around here," my gardener replied. "I'm surprised you haven't seen him before, Monsieur Borel, because he takes a stroll on this very road every morning at nine. He's an old gentleman with white hair, dressed all in black. There's something odd about him. The farmers think he's some kind of warlock, that he's got powers... Some are afraid of him, they think he has the evil eye... They avoid him like the plague..."

"Bah!" I said, dismissing the notion entirely.

After having shaken all the bits of glass loose from my clothes, I left the gazebo and returned home.

Still, I found myself distracted for the rest of the evening... I could not concentrate and play well. I attributed my sudden fit of nerves to the shock I had undergone and decided to retire for the night.

When I walked into my bedroom, I immediately noticed that the mantelpiece mirror was broken from one side to the other, and my portrait–a pastel watercolor that depicted me in my twenties–had fallen from the wall and lay on the floor at the foot of my bed.

"That was quite an explosion," Marcel, my valet, remarked. "I don't think I've ever heard anything like it before. Some in the village may have been injured. If you don't mind my saying so, Monsieur Borel, I think the Doctor owes it to you to replace your beautiful mirror and the frame of your portrait."

"Yes, maybe, we'll see... Pull the curtains and turn down the bed, please."

Marcel did as he was told, then his services no longer required, left the room.

For a quarter of an hour, I paced the room, smoking a cigarette, unable to relax. Finally, I went to bed, and turned off my bedside lamp.

Strangely, I, who normally fell asleep immediately as soon as my head touched the pillow, could not do so that night.

I kept turning in bed, my mind returning to the explosion, the hangar, and that mysterious Doctor who inspired so much fear among the villagers, and whom I tried to visualize in my mind.

Then, it occurred to me that, perhaps, he too may have been buried under the debris, and I began to worry and feel sorry about the old man.

This was becoming a ridiculous obsession.

At long last, I fell asleep.

But not long after, I was suddenly awakened by a small creaking sound... Almost a slithering noise. I breathlessly listened to the darkness, then silently sat up in my bed, but could no longer hear anything. The room was in complete silence.

"I must have been dreaming," I thought.

Still, as I felt heavy-headed, I got up and opened the window.

Outside, a bat flew past and disappeared into a tree.

In the distance, a silvery mist floated over the woods, lit up by a bright, shining moon.

I turned my eyes towards the village... A small bluish light, like that of embers half-buried under ashes in a fireplace, shone where one of Doctor Omega's hangars used to stand. I assumed it was some wreckage from the explosion that was still burning.

I walked around my room, feeling the need to reassure myself by touching the familiar furniture and objects that darkness now made look strange and alien to my eyes. Once completely satisfied that all was as it should be, I closed the window and returned to my bed.

How long did I sleep that time? I could not tell...

Again, I woke up with a strange feeling of unease. I felt as if I was suffocating... There was a great weight on my chest...

I leaped up, and distinctly heard the sound of something falling onto the floor...

Fear filled my whole being... A numbness invaded my mind... A strange paralysis overtook my entire body... My heart was beating a mad drumbeat... I shivered as if from great cold and felt my skin crawl...

I could no longer doubt it.

There was someone–or something–in my room. Of this, I was now certain!

I remained perfectly still under my covers for what seemed to be an eternity. Then, slowly, I raised my head and looked around.

Everything was dark and silent.

I was just starting to regain my composure, and had found a thousand reasons to banish my fears, when another horrible sight turned my blood to ice.

At the foot of my bed, out of the darkness, two shining yellow eyes were looking at me, two burning orbs that seemed enormous.

Mad terror returned as suddenly as it had left... My teeth shook... I totally lost my mind... My imagination ran wild and I started seeing more visions of horror.

The furniture in my room seemed to move and a strange light appeared out of nowhere, revealing a terrifying figure.

A diabolical being, a creature from hell itself, stood only a few feet away from me. He was a tall, elderly man, all dressed in black, with slick white hair pulled back, except for a rebellious lock on his forehead. He was smiling an all-knowing, mephisthophelean smile, such as Milton could have given to his Lucifer. His eyes were of a penetrating blue; they never wavered and transfixed me with their inhuman, timeless evil, just as the snake holds its prey motionless by the pure power of its gaze.

I heard the morbid, clickety noise of bones rattling, which I dimly realized were the sound of my own teeth chattering.

Then, on the broken mirror above my mantelpiece, a word slowly appeared in letters of fire, written by an invisible hand. The word: Omega!

I do not recall what happened next, for I simply passed out.

When I awoke, Marcel was pulling the curtains to let the morning sun into the room. I had not even heard him knock at the door and come in. I rubbed my eyes, blinking at the sharpness of the light that fell straight across my bed. I looked around the room in a daze. I examined the ceiling, the walls, the furniture. Except for the broken mirror–virgin of any words–everything was perfectly normal.

Still, I did not feel completely at ease, and as my servant was about to leave, I found some excuse to ask him to stay. I did not want to be alone.

As I got up, I noticed a big, black tomcat sleeping peacefully at the foot of my bed. I had never seen it before, but presumably it had been scared by the explosion, and had found refuge in my home, and liking its comfort, had decided to stay.

At last, I broke into a smile, for that explained the mysteries of the night... Now I understood what had happened... The pressure on my chest... The sound of something falling on the floor... The two yellow eyes looking at me out of the darkness... Yes, everything made perfect sense!

The cat had decided to sleep on me, as most cats like to do, and my overactive imagination had done the rest. Everything I had seen afterwards was nothing more than a half-conscious dream, inspired by the events of the day.

I had gone to sleep thinking about the mysterious Doctor Omega, and my feverish mind had created an entire fantastic story out of night shapes and dream stuff, as sometimes occurs when a particularly striking event has happened to you during the day, and you still carry its vivid remembrance with you when you fall asleep.

I got up, took my morning bath, and felt almost normal. Yet, a few hours later, my trepidation had returned, and I again felt nervous and irritable. The images of the mysterious Doctor continued to haunt my mind.

I tried playing my violin, but found I still could not concentrate.

I made a mess of almost all the harmonics, and my bow, poorly assured in my hand, merely screeched on the strings.

It was pathetic.

I felt so angry that I stamped my foot, and decided to go out.

I returned to the gazebo and leaned on the small stone wall that overlooked the main road.

I was angry... Angry at myself for the nightmares... Angry to have become so obsessed by that Doctor Omega who should have meant nothing to me.

What strange fate could be compelling me to take an interest in that man?

Some modern experts in psychic sciences would perhaps explain my state of mind by resorting to telepathy or thought transference, but there was nothing between Doctor Omega and myself that could give rise to such explanations. How could two beings who had never met, who are ignorant of each other, be psychically connected?

There I was in my musings, when suddenly I heard the sound of footsteps approaching. I looked up, leaned over the wall, and could not repress my surprise.

Doctor Omega–seemingly unharmed and unaffected by the horrible tragedy of the day before–was walking on the road.

Now that I could get a good look at him, I realized he was just as my servants had described him. An old man, dressed in black. He was tallish, wrapped in a cloak and wore a fur hat and a long, striped scarf. His silver hair was slick and long in the back, with a rebellious lock tilting upward on his forehead. His eyes blazed with intelligence, and a prominent, beaky nose gave his face an arrogant and somewhat aristocratic look.

He was using a walking stick, and sometimes made strange figures with it on the ground, although without ever slowing down. I was close enough that I could hear the crunching sound the leaves made beneath his feet. It was obvious that he had not seen me observing him from my vantage post.

I was about to say hello and introduce myself when he took a sharp turn to the left and took a small path that was a local short-cut through the woods.

For a second, I thought of shouting for him to stop; I was just about to do it, but was held back by a sense of propriety.

·I could not properly hail a man to whom I had never been formally introduced.

That sudden apparition, far from appeasing my curiosity, only made it more intense.

The old man who, under any other circumstances, would not have even caught my attention, now seemed to me an otherworldly figure... a living mystery...

He walked calmly, like one of the figures in Dante's *Inferno* who crossed the flames without feeling their heat, as if he was imbued with a strange power that placed him outside the reach of everyday life.

How could he otherwise go out for a morning stroll when he had almost decimated an entire village the night before?

During the rest of the day, I fell prey to the blackest of moods, and my servants who were used to my easy manners, were surprised to have to endure my criticisms for the most capricious of reasons.

Even my darling Stradivarius had been displaced in my mind. Doctor Omega had become the sole focus of my attention.

His appearance, which I had now beheld, looked strikingly like the figure that I had seen in my dream. My servants had provided me with a sketchy description; yet, the similarities were astounding.

How could that be possible? Could my dream have somehow tapped into a deeper truth? Could my fevered imagination have revealed some unfathomable secret?

My curiosity now reached its paroxysm.

I had to meet the mysterious old man... I had to speak to him, if only for an instant... I had to find out what strange work he was doing in those hangars.

I made up my mind quickly.

The next day, I intended to confront the Doctor during his morning walk.

As I feared I would experience another dreadful nightmare if I slept, I did not go to bed at all that night.

I simply sat in an armchair, and left the lights on.

The night seemed endless.

Finally, a wan trickle of daylight shone through the curtains–dawn had come.

I dressed myself without Marcel's assistance, and quickly left the house, crossed the park and slipped through a back gate that let out onto the fields behind my property.

It was daft to go out so early, since the man I sought did not normally make his rounds until nine o'clock. But I was fretting impatiently, and could not have stayed idly at home another minute. I had to do something, anything, to distract myself.

As soon as I had left the fields that bordered the back of my property, I found that my steps were leading me, almost against my will, in the very direction that I had meant to avoid.

Even though I took detours, stopped to look at my surroundings, and otherwise found any excuse to while away the time, an unknown force insistently pushed me towards the main road that led to the hollow at the other end of the village–the home of Doctor Omega!

I resigned myself, and soon I reached my destination. Before me, the road stretched on at an angle exaggerated by the perspective of the hollow, and under the rays of the dawning sun, it resembled a ribbon of melted gold.

Not too far from where I stood was a compact mass of smoking debris, made up of large beams, wooden planks, cast iron work and other strange metals partially melted together.

The same strange bluish light I had seen during the night shone over parts of these ruins, and I thought it must have been the result of some acid or chemical reaction.

From where I stood, I even imagined that some of the wreckage looked like burned-out bodies, stretching their blackened arms towards the sky in silent prayer.

But as I stepped closer, I recognized that these "bodies" were only small cylindrical tanks, still affixed to pieces of charred timber.

In the midst of the destruction, an odd item emerged, relatively unscathed. A strange hexagonal column, with a sphere on top of it that might have been a globe, except that it had been so darkened by the smoke that it now looked like a giant billiard ball, sadly abandoned by some gargantuan player.

Further on, I saw partially burned books spread out on the ground, and a few other items that must have been blown clear by the explosion: a top hat, a red bathrobe still hanging from the hook of a coat hanger, and a musical instrument that looked like a recorder...

At the epicenter of the explosion itself, the ground was cratered, torn apart... Some shrubberies had been chopped away, as if cut off with shears.

I was lost in my thoughts at the contemplation of this dreadful scene of devastation, when suddenly I heard a voice from behind me.

"Quite an explosion, eh?"

I turned around hurriedly and found myself face to face with Doctor Omega.

He saluted me with a curt nod; his face was smiling benevolently, but there was a cold and almost inhuman light of amusement in his eyes that betrayed his apparent geniality, something chilling and cruel that sent a shiver down my spine.

His words were clipped, delivered in that perfect French that school principals have been trained to use since the Revolution, with the same undertone of condescension. Yet, I could not help but feel that he was anything but French.

"What do you want, young man?" he asked.

"What do I want? Er... Nothing... I didn't mean to trespass. It's just that... I'm..." I blurted out. "I'm glad there weren't any victims... Were there?"

The Doctor did not seem to hear my question.

I grew bolder.

"You must be a scientist... An inventor perhaps?"

He nodded distractedly. I could see I was losing his attention.

I wanted to ask him what he was trying to invent, but I did not dare.

Yet I could not let him go; I had to know.

Suddenly, I had a brilliant inspiration.

"I'm an inventor too," I said.

The Doctor looked at me with his penetrating gaze, and I felt he was seeing through my fleshy envelope and peering directly into my soul. He must have been satisfied with his examination, because a thin smile slowly crossed his face. Putting his hand on my shoulder, he suddenly asked me a most unexpected question:

"Are you courageous, young man?"

"Why would you want to know?" I asked, suddenly concerned.

"You'll find out soon enough... I want to know if you're courageous."

"Of course, I am," I said, straightening my posture and adopting what I thought was a brave expression.

"Have you even been scared in your life?"

"Never!" I lied shamelessly.

"Good. You may be the man I'm looking for. What's your name?"

"Denis Borel."

"Well then, Borel, come and see me tonight. Nine sharp."

"Here?" I said, pointing at the other hangar, which had been left mostly unscathed by the explosion.

"Yes, here. Use the side door entrance and ring the bell. Ring several times, because I can become very absorbed by my work, and I may not hear you the first time. Good-bye now, Borel. I shall see you later."

The Doctor shook my hand.

That contact made a strange and unpleasant impression on me.

It felt–odd. As if someone had just walked on my grave, as the old saying goes.

As I walked away, I was mentally reviewing my encounter with Doctor Omega.

"The Devil take me if I go to that appointment," I thought. "The man is clearly insane.

"Besides, if he wanted to tell me what he did, he could have done so then and there. Hah! If he thinks I'm going to go to that shack of his in the middle of the night, he is grossly mistaken.

"I don't care to spend another minute with that lunatic!"

Once back home, I first helped myself to a hearty breakfast, and then I played violin for two hours, my mind now free of any morbid curiosity.

During the afternoon, I essayed myself on Bazzini's *Dance of the Goblins*, and it seemed to me that my pizzicati almost rivaled those of the great Jan Kubelik.

Still, at night fall, my obsession returned–in force.

The conversation of the morning was still fresh in my mind and, going through it one more time, I now questioned whether the Doctor was as insane as I earlier had thought him to be.

"After all," I thought, "his handshake was perfectly normal, reassuring even. It was cold outside, that's all. And his eyes were not cruel. They're just a very piercing blue.

"His gestures, too, were not those of a lunatic. Crazy people are very brusque, uncontrolled in their movements. Doctor Omega was very precise, exacting even. Yes, he is an eccentric, but then again, so am I!

"People who spend their lives doing scientific research have earned the right to be eccentric. Nothing estranges you from the daily routine of normal life like an unbridled passion for research.

"And, scientists are not like everyone else either. They have wonderful, brilliant brains, too complex to be understood by ordinary people who like to quickly stick labels on anything that's beyond their comprehension.

"Do I have the right to call Doctor Omega mad before I have judged his work? What if he is a real genius?"

Engrossed in such soliloquies, the dinner hour came quickly.

I barely touched the dishes offered to me, eating only two eggs, with half a glass of wine.

When I got up from the table, I was more troubled and undecided than ever.

I sat down in my library to again ponder my options.

If I did not go to the Doctor's appointment, I would be forever branded a coward in his eyes, and he would laugh at me, or worse, every time we again met.

On the other hand, I was much too interested in the man and his work to not take advantage of the opportunity he had offered me; here was my chance to finally learn the truth.

One thing, however, still concerned me: Why did he ask me if I had ever been afraid?

"Bah!" I said to myself, "I shall see for myself!"

Eight-thirty had just rung. I got up and began to prepare myself to go out when another thought stopped me in my tracks.

What if the Doctor was planning to use me as a guinea pig for some ungodly experiment of his, like the mad Doctor Caresco, whose crimes had made headlines a few years earlier? What if he was indeed a dangerous lunatic?

"By God, I know how to defend myself," I thought, and pulled my Smith & Wesson revolver from the desk drawer.

"I'll see what his intentions are right away. If they're in the least chancy, I'll find an excuse to leave at once.

"And even if he tries to stop me, I can escape from his clutches. By Jove, I'm young and strong, and he's just an old man. Plus I'm armed. He won't be much of a challenge."

I stepped out of the library, and grabbed my rain coat because the weather looked stormy. I slipped the gun into my jacket pocket.

My servant, who saw my gesture, looked frightened.

"Monsieur Borel..." he asked, after some hesitation.

"Yes, Marcel?"

"You've never gone out at night, not once since I've been in your service."

"I have an appointment," I said.

And then, out of a mischievous sense of bravado, I added:

"An appointment with Doctor Omega."

Marcel rolled his eyes almost as if I had mentioned the Devil.

·"You're... going to meet that old warlock? Oh, sir, please, be careful! That man is capable of anything! This afternoon, in the village, they told me frightening things about him... If only you knew..."

I shrugged and left the house. I was outwardly calm even though, inside, I was deeply troubled.

As soon as I reached the main road, I began walking briskly, hitting the road sharply with my heels, louder than necessary.

Fat, stormy clouds rolled in, obscuring the sky. I could not see anything further than ten feet away.

After I had crossed the village, the moon made a brief appearance between the clouds. My shadow then appeared on the ground... A huge, gigantic shadow that twisted and turned before me.

As I passed a lonely farm house at the edge of the hollow, a dog began howling and I shivered nervously.

Was I in danger of losing my courage?

I got a grip on myself, pulled my cap down, and steadfastly walked towards the hangar, which had only one window lit up.

Standing before the darkened building, I still hesitated for a second. Then, grabbing the chain hanging to the right of the door, I pulled sharply.

It is impossible for me to express the effect that the tinny ring of the bell had on me; a dead man to whom Fate would have granted the ability to hear his funeral bells would not have been more moved than I was in that instant.

Soon enough, a light shone through a small peephole in the door; it opened and I again found myself face to face with Doctor Omega.

This time, his head was bare, and that rebellious lock of white hair atop his forehead looked like a crest. He stood, silhouetted against the light, an impressive figure in spite of his age.

Watching him, then and there, I could not help but remember my awful nightmare, and my legs nearly went out from under me.

I involuntarily took a step back, almost as if to flee, but the Doctor ushered me in and quickly locked the door behind me. The lock looked like a box to me, but it made a buzzing sound as it clicked shut. The Doctor emitted a dry chuckle as he explained:

"A trionic lock. It's an ingenious mechanism. And yet very simple..." Then he added:

"We're protected from any indiscretion now... Follow me upstairs, young man."

The scientist went up a flight of stairs, holding a copper lantern that projected an unusually white light of a type I had never seen before, and which cast large and well-delineated shadows on the walls.

I discretely checked that my gun was still in my jacket pocket, and a brief touch of its handle restored my confidence.

The Doctor was climbing the stairs in a manner surprisingly spry for a man of his age; indeed I found it difficult to keep up with him.

Once we reached a narrow landing, he opened a door sporting another of those strange locks of his, and stepped aside to allow me to enter.

"Come in, young man, come in."

I do not know why, but when he called me "young man," I felt much more than the difference of a score and a few more years in our respective ages. I feared to read in those words more than a casual expression of condescension, but a cruel and ironic mockery.

I entered a large room, all made of acajou wood, with circular alcoves cut into the walls. To the right of the door there was a single window, tall and narrow, looking like a medieval castle's arrow slit or *meurtrière*.

At the other end of the room, behind a transparent door that looked like it was made of quartz, was another, smaller, room, a laboratory whose walls appeared to have been reinforced with steel plates as thick as those of a battleship.

Inside was a spherical container from which radiated a pulsating light that alternated between blight silver and blue. The container was embedded in a small column that was itself resting at the center of a larger hexagonal machine, the purpose of which I could not divine.

The column was either made of light, or of some material that had the same properties as light, as it shone so brightly it hurt the eyes to look at it. It was going up and down in a repeating pattern, and its movements seemed echoed by the pulsations of light emanating from the sphere.

"Please sit down," said the Doctor, handing me an antique chair.

Since in spite of his invitation, I remained standing, he insisted:

"Sit down, Borel. We have much to talk about, you and I, eh?"

I obeyed without a second thought, and the old man sat down across from me.

Half of his face was in the shadows, and the other half brightly lit by the light from the laboratory. It seemed inhumanly pallid to me.

I noticed that, despite the play of light and darkness, his eyes shone brightly and I could clearly see them sparkling in his face. Every time his gaze fell on me, I repressed a shudder.

Outside, the storm had broken, and I heard the gale of the wind and the pounding of the rain.

I also heard the distant groaning of the trees, and the creaking sound of a rusty wind vane on the roof of the hangar, rotating madly in the wind.

The Doctor smiled his mirthless smile, and leaned towards me.

"Much to talk about indeed... You probably want to know why I asked you to come, don't you?"

"Well, I confess that... yes," I replied.

The Doctor rubbed his hands, then threw me a look that had such a cunning gleam in it that it briefly rekindled my fears.

"I am looking for a man of courage to be my companion on a fantastic voyage–the word is not too strong– an extraordinary journey that I have long labored to make possible."

Seeing the expression of bafflement on my face, he sighed:

"Perhaps things will become clearer if I tell you that I have been working for many years on the synthesis of a new element... You know what an element is, eh?"

I nodded, and satisfied, he continued:

"This element... You could think of it as a metal of sorts... A living metal... It's not part of the quadridimensional structure of space and time as we know it... It... I guess you could say that it *repels* them..."

"Repels space?"

"And time."

I shook my head as if to indicate my understanding or even my admiration, but in fact the more Doctor Omega explained his discovery, the more I thought he was indeed a lunatic. However, I thought that his madness was harmless, and if I did not challenge him, I would have nothing to fear.

In fact, I would have felt completely at ease except that, from time to time, the Doctor turned around to check on the progress of whatever was going on in the laboratory behind him.

Several times during our conversation, he got up and walked to the glass door to check on the machine, tweak some controls, or take a reading from an instrument on a panel located next to it.

His actions had piqued my curiosity, a fact that had not escaped his attention. Reading in my eyes the question I had not dared ask, he volunteered:

"You're wondering what's going on in that room, eh?"

I could not deny it.

"Since I judge you to be made of the right stuff, young man, I shall tell you. The element I spoke about can only be synthesized under extreme conditions of pressure and heat... Millions of degrees... A pressure that could crush stars..."

Hearing these words, I felt a bead of cold sweat trickle down my back. Was he truly mad, or playing with forces that could...? Suddenly, I experienced a revelation.

The Doctor must have read my mind, for he confirmed my awful suspicion.

"Yes, it's a process just like that one which caused the explosion of yesterday. It's a very delicate process. Where... I come from... we manufactured this element in outer space so dangerous a process it is... But here, I do not have that luxury, so I had to improvise..."

He again got up to monitor the pulsating sphere. The up and down movement of the central column had slowed somewhat, and the bluish light had dimmed.

"I think we're almost done..."

Then noticing my worried countenance, he snapped:

"Don't fret, Borel. The dangerous part is over. Come here, I'll show you something that will remove any doubts that may yet linger in your mind."

The Doctor walked to a closet, which he opened. It was surprisingly large inside, and I saw that it contained what looked like thick metal sheets on a row of shelves, but made of a metal as I had never before seen. Its color seemed to vary from dull silver to shiny blue, and its texture reminded me of mercury. It was hard to focus one's eyes on it as its very presence appeared to shift from solid and metallic to something that did not entirely belong to our reality, like a rainbow that is there and yet not there at the same time.

"Grab one of those plates," ordered the Doctor.

I did not want to defy the old man's will, but the metal sheets looked very heavy.

"I don't think I could lift one," I said, tentatively touching the metal with one finger. It felt cold under my hand, and perfectly normal, except for an almost imperceptible vibration that anyone but a violinist would have missed.

"Give it a try," said the Doctor with a smile.

I grabbed the huge metal sheet with two hands and prepared to use all my strength to lift it when, to my surprise, I discovered that it weighed less than a feather. In fact, carried by the momentum of my movement, the sheet rose in the air, and I had to exert pressure to bring it down and put it back on the shelf.

"What do you think now, eh?"

"This is... incredible! Wonderful! Amazing! It's a miracle!"

My sudden transformation from doubtful skeptic to enthusiastic follower brought a smile of satisfaction to Doctor Omega's face.

I now looked at this man with unbound awe. It seemed to me that there was something truly superhuman about him. The white-haired old man who had previously seemed crazy and terrifying had suddenly turned into a demi-god before my eyes.

"You've seen but a ridiculous fraction of what this metal is capable of. Ships were made of it. Very special ships. Ships unbound by the shackles of space and time. I've long searched to duplicate the ability to make this wondrous substance, and build a ship I could truly call my own. Now I'm close to achieving that dream. Would you accompany me on the maiden voyage of such a ship?"

What I had just beheld had banished any notion of hesitation from my mind. I was fascinated... astonished... almost entranced...

"Doctor! I'm ready to follow you anywhere! To the ends of the Earth, if you will!"

"Oh, I think we'll go further than that," he said with a smile.

Before I had time to ponder the meaning of his last statement, I heard a loud groaning and wheezing sound come from the laboratory. In spite of myself, remembering the explosion, I again was seized by fear.

"Don't worry, young man," said the Doctor, noting my concern. "This means that the synthesis is almost over... Then, I'll have the final piece I need... After it's cooled down sufficiently, of course."

"So there's no danger?"

"Not at this time."

Then, the scientist continued calmly:

"I need someone to accompany me on my journey... I have a granddaughter, but she is studying in Paris at the *Pension Clavel*... Besides, this may be too dangerous for her... I have a strong and reliable assistant, but I'm afraid he's not a man of learning. I need an intelligent and educated companion who can document my journey... To take notes... To write down what I will tell him... Keeping records is important, eh?"

"A secretary?"

"Yes, you might call it that."

"I understand," I said, but I was again distracted by the wheezing noise that kept emanating from the laboratory, in an increasingly threatening fashion, or so I thought.

Perhaps it was my imagination, but I thought I was hearing the sphere crack under the unimaginable pressure, fracture and explode, spilling the molten metal everywhere, killing us both in the process.

I tried hiding my fears, and either I succeeded better than before, or the Doctor was more distracted, because he did not appear to notice that my heart was thumping wildly in my chest, and that, despite the apparent serenity of my face, a thin sheet of sweat now shone on my features.

"I think that, er, maybe you should take another look at the synthesis," I finally brought myself to say in a timid voice.

But Doctor Omega seemed lost in his thoughts and did not hear me.

Finally, the meaning of my words penetrated his mind, for he turned to look towards the laboratory, but then, just at that moment, we heard a loud, banging noise from the ground floor. The sound of a door being slammed shut... or opened.

"What's that?" said the old man, suddenly aware and sporting that air of suspicion he had worn when we had first met. "Who could have opened my trionic lock? Impossible!" Then, turning towards me, "Wait here! It won't take me more than a second or two. I must go and check..."

"I'll come with you," I shouted, not wanting to stay alone in this mad laboratory.

But before I had time to move, with surprising spryness, he had already left the room. The door had shut behind him, and when I tried to open it, it refused to budge. I did not know how to work that amazing "trionic lock" of his–no doubt, another invention of that brilliant man–and I realized that I had become a prisoner. From the other side, I heard him rush down the stairs. Then, there was the ominous sound of a fall, a crash, the Doctor's voice, high-pitched and almost indignant, then silence.

I wondered what had happened.

I was stuck to the spot, worried, deeply troubled.

Meanwhile, the wheezing noise from the laboratory had only gone up in intensity. Its stridency and speed made it sound like the rapid breathing of some kind of mythical beast.

I tried the door again, but the lock held. In a desperate move, I even shoved myself against it, but it remained impervious to my repeated blows.

Downstairs, Doctor Omega must have been conscious and heard my attempts, for I caught his muffled voice, but could not make up what he was saying. So I kneeled down to the floor, put my ear to the wood, and then was able to hear his words clearly.

"The synthesis! It's out of control!"

I knew it! What I'd feared most had happened. I was going to die here, in another explosion, and Doctor Omega was unable to come and rescue me.

Gathering all my strength, I rushed back to the control panel near the quartz door, where I had seen the Doctor perform his manipulations before. Inside the laboratory, the synthesis indeed appeared to be out of control, as the column was now moving in a rapid staccato, and the coruscating energies emanating from the sphere were unleashing wave after wave of sharp, blinding light, against the din of that infernal wheezing sound.

The control panel was deceptively simple, with only a few buttons and dials, whose indications meant nothing to me. I did not know what to do, but I saw a large, red button that conveyed in my mind the notion of an alarm bell. So, with little hesitation, I decided that I had nothing to lose, and pressed it. Maybe that would be my salvation?

Instead, I cursed under my breath, because it seemed that I had only hastened my impending demise!

The sphere seemed to bulge, ready to crack under some all-powerful inner pressure, like a dragon's egg ready to burst and release the monster within... The wheezing became a deafening high-pitched whistle... On one of the dials, the needle jumped up sharply, which could only be a bad sign... The light drowned the room under its stroboscopic glare... I felt, or perhaps imagined, the heat rising up significantly...

I wanted to scream, but discovered that I could not. My throat had become paralyzed... My tongue stuck to the plate of my mouth...

I knew it was nearly the end...

I stepped back to the other end of the room, trying to find some protection behind the sparse furniture, looking haggardly at the light, and finally collapsing to my knees on the floor, hiding my face in my hands...

I could not breathe... Fear gripped my chest... The last vestiges of reason were snuffed out of my mind as my consciousness ebbed away, and I fainted.

Chapter Two
A New Element

When I came to, the first thing I saw was a large man looking at me with a broad smile on his bearded face.

I looked back at him in puzzlement, and was about to ask who he was, when he beat me to the punch.

"Do you feel all right, sir?" he asked. "Lucky that I got here just in time, or else we could have all been blown to Kingdom come. Where is the Doctor?"

"Downstairs," I replied, marveling at the man's calm composure.

"What? He left you here alone? Without telling you how to stop the synthesizer if it went into overdrive?"

"He thought he was leaving for only a minute. He intended to return immediately. He went downstairs to check on the door, but didn't come back. I thought he fell, or had an accident."

"I've got to go and see what's happened to him then," said the big man with a worried expression on his face.

"I'll come with you."

I got up, somewhat painfully for my muscles were aching, and followed him. The door was now opened, as he obviously knew his way around trionic locks. On the landing, I saw another door leading into a corridor, out of which the man had obviously rushed when he had heard the alarming sounds emanating from the laboratory.

We walked down the stairs to the front door. The Doctor was nowhere in sight. The big man examined the lock carefully.

"Now I get it! That lock is broken! It was pushed open by the storm, and I bet the Doctor got locked out trying to fix it. It was bound to happen sooner or later. These trionic locks aren't nearly as reliable as he makes them sound. Give me a good wooden bolt anytime..."

The man pulled out an instrument that might have been a screwdriver, even though I could hear it emit a low buzzing sound. With it, he did something to the lock, I did not see what, because it suddenly snapped opened.

We stepped outside, but again saw no one.

"Where is the Doctor?" asked the big man.

"I heard him shout at me earlier," I said. "Maybe he went around the building looking for another entrance?"

The man put his hands around his mouth like a hearing trumpet and shouted, "Doctor! Doctor!"

Then we heard a muffled groan coming from around the corner of the hangar.

We rushed over to find Doctor Omega lying on the ground, barely conscious. He had been hit in the head by one of the pieces of wood sent flying by the storm. He seemed angry, and there was a red gash on his forehead. His clothes were dirty with debris.

The big man tried to help the Doctor to his feet, but the old man pushed him away testily. I ventured to speak, but was rebuffed. My companion fared no better when he inquired about the old man's condition.

"Enough, Fred! I told you that I'm fine. It's nothing serious."

Then, he seemed to calm himself, and turned towards me:

"Did you stop the synthesizer?"

"Don't worry, Doctor. I did it. And just in time too," said Fred.

The scientist was obviously relieved and let out one of his dry chuckles.

"It must have given you quite a fright, eh, Borel?"

Desirous to live up to my earlier self-portrayal of bravery, which I had so given, I answered calmly.

"Not really. I tried to fix the problem, but when I realized it was hopeless, I just lay down on the floor and waited to die."

The Doctor took me at my word, but I could see a mischievous gleam in Fred's eye. He, better than anyone else, knew that I was no hero.

Then, the Doctor confirmed the big man's scenario as to what had happened. An especially powerful gust of wind had broken the lock and slammed the hangar door open. Rushing to close it, the Doctor had fallen down the steps. Still dizzy, he had tried to repair the lock, but instead had only succeeded in locking himself out. As I had surmised, he had tried to warn me, but just then been hit by the flying debris before he could issue any more instructions.

With all that had happened, dawn was now almost upon us.

"After such an eventful night," the Doctor concluded, "we both need some rest. Why don't you enjoy my hospitality and stay here a bit longer?"

The notion of having to walk several kilometers to return to my home was suddenly very unappealing, and I gratefully accepted Doctor Omega's offer.

He led me back inside and, through a series of corridors, took me to a sparsely furnished room with a couple of chairs, a small bed, and a few blankets.

"You can rest here," he said. "It's almost five. I'll have you wakened at noon. That will give you seven hours' sleep. Judging by your face, I think you'll need them."

Indeed, I did. The strong emotions of the day had exhausted me. I felt totally drained. I collapsed on the bed without even taking my clothes off, and fell asleep immediately.

I was in deep slumber, and had been for a while, when I was suddenly jolted awake by loud shouting coming from outside. I tried to catch a few words in the cacophony, but I could only hear the din of the mob mixed with threats and curses.

The door opened and Doctor Omega came in, followed by Fred, who was armed with a big stick.

"Do you hear that?" said the Doctor. "They're threatening to break down my door! They're uttering death threats! And the gendarme is doing nothing to stop them! I saw him among them! Ah, I rue the day I came here, among these savages!"

I shared his concern and opened the window to better assess the situation.

As soon as the crowd saw me, the nature of their utterances changed:

"There he is! He's safe!"

And then I understood! At the forefront of the crowd were Marcel and Pierre, my gardener.

I burst out laughing, and turning towards the Doctor, I explained:

"You don't have a good reputation among the locals. They're superstitious peasants. They think you're a warlock. My servants knew that I was coming here, and when I didn't return last night, they thought you'd killed me!"

From my window, I spoke to the crowd and appeased them. In a loud and clear voice, I told them that Doctor Omega was not what they thought.

"He's a great man," I shouted. "A wonderful scientist. Soon, you will marvel at his incredible inventions. Show him respect, my friends! Shower him with praise! It's an honor for this village to have him living amongst us. Soon, people will come from all over France, nay, from all over the world, to see him!"

Either I was a better speaker than I thought, or they looked forward to a long line of wealthy visitors, but in any event, they applauded me with all their strength. It sounded like the drum roll of rain on a tin roof.

Fred nudged the Doctor forward, and in spite of his testiness, he stood at the window and waved at the crowd. The cheers only became louder.

Watching him, I guessed that this was a man not used to public acclaim; he was not the type to seek fame, preferring to work quietly behind the scenes.

He said a few words, which I don't think the crowd heard, but which they greeted with even more enthusiasm.

It had taken only a few minutes to turn this social outcast, mistrusted by the simple-minded natives, into a local hero. It is one of the most striking peculiarities of crowds, good and bad, to be so capable of changing their minds on a collective whim.

When the applause stopped, I summoned Marcel who was still standing just outside the hangar, and gave him some instructions. Then, turning towards Doctor Omega, whose face was filled with self-satisfaction, I said:

"Come with me, Doctor. I'm inviting you for breakfast."

After a slight hesitation, he agreed and, a few minutes later, the Doctor, Fred and I took off towards my house.

The crowd parted respectfully, and followed us all the way home.

Once there, I had four caskets of my best wine brought up from the cellar, and shared them liberally with the villagers.

That generous gesture reinforced their positive mood towards the Doctor, and the esteem they already felt towards me.

At the end of our meal, perhaps as a result of drinking some of my Spanish wine, with great moderation, I rush to add, unlike Fred, the Doctor became very chatty.

"When you saw me for the first time, I must have seemed to you a rather odd type of fellow, mustn't I, Borel?"

"Er, I never..."

"Yes, yes, you can admit it now. Say it. You thought I must have been quite a lunatic, eh?"

"Well, you did seem somewhat oblivious of the consequences of the explosion..."

"But that wasn't the case, you see? I knew that it had injured no one because I had Fred immediately make inquiries. And I'm sure you must have thought all my talk about new elements was complete balderdash–that is, until you saw my laboratory, eh?"

"I'll admit that it seemed so... fantastic..."

"Well, since you've agreed to accompany me on my journey, the least I can do is satisfy your curiosity, but you must give me your word that anything I tell you shall remain strictly between us."

I swore that my lips would be sealed, and no one would hear a word from me of what he was about to tell me.

"As you surmised, I'm not from here. I'm from... another country... whose name, for the moment, I cannot reveal. Suffice it to say that it is far from France. In my native land, I was a scientist. I'd spent more years than I care to remember studying minute samples of mysterious new elements that a fellow scientist had brought back from an exploratory journey inside a black hole..."

"A... *black hole*?"

"Surely you've heard of Newton's laws of gravity, eh? Well, massive bodies can generate such strong gravity that nothing, not even light, can escape their grip. We call such objects black holes. They're entrances to a continuum that exists outside of space and time as we know it. But I see that I'm losing you. Just accept that what lies within a black hole has physical properties very different from those of our natural universe.

"So, as I was saying, I spent a long time studying the exotic elements brought back by my colleague... validium, chronodyne... and a new element which I dubbed *stellite*. One of the fascinating properties of stellite is that it's a pandimensional metal. It will not naturally remain in our physical universe. Think, if you will, of a small empty ball full of air, like a tennis ball. If you deposit it in a bucket of water, it will float. If you want it to be submerged, you'll have to push it down. And if you let go of it, it will quickly bob back up to the surface. Water, in this example, is our own quadri-dimensional space-time continuum, and stellite is the ball. Do you see?"

"Er... yes, yes, I do," I replied, even though most of his explanations were entirely incomprehensible to my scientifically untrained mind.

"Stellite offered an array of tantalizing possibilities to my people who, at the time, were still great explorers; we were ready to embark on a new era of travel, with no barriers standing in our way, not even physical ones. Stellite was the key to building ships that could endure the incredible pressures of the type of travel of which our engineers dreamed. But I had the only sample of stellite ever brought back to our universe, and to do even that much had almost cost my colleague his life.

"Now your own Lavoisier–a wonderfully keen mind, sadly cut down in his prime by your revolution–spent much of his own brief life studying chemical compounds, trying to break them down into simpler, basic substances, which he called elements, and describing their composition by mass and heat properties... I did the same thing, except that in my laboratory, it was matter itself that I broke down into its components: solids into atoms, atoms into particles, and particles into quarks and chronons..."

Noticing my bafflement, he pointed at the bust of Mozart which decorated my mantelpiece.

"Do you see that statue? What if I told you that I could break it down to the minutest grain of sand that makes up the stone out of which it was carved? Then what if I could spread each and every of these millions of grains of sand on this table to understand how they came to be together and make up that bust? And then, what if I could take another pile of sand and replicate the positions of its grains, just to make more busts like that one? Well, doing all this would still be nothing compared to the immensity of the task I had embarked upon when I had decided to study stellite, and discover if it could be artificially manufactured in our factories.

"My initial experiments were nothing short of catastrophic–the explosion of the other day was a firecracker compared to the nearly apocalyptic results of my first attempt at synthesizing stellite. In fact, as I think I told you, my people quickly decided to move our facilities to a place where we no longer risked endangering our citizenry.

"I'll spare you the stories of endless nights spent poring over reams of calculations, the many useless experiments that produced nothing but grief and skepticism from others. Many in my place would have become discouraged. Yet, I persisted, because I knew that someday I would succeed, I had to succeed, there was no other possibility, you see?

"As is often the case with breakthrough scientific discoveries, it was pure chance–or so it seemed–that eventually allowed me to stumble upon the key equations I needed in order to develop a safe process capable of recreating stellite in a laboratory under artificial conditions. I came across the idea in a very old book, something not unlike your own alchemy tomes dating back to the 12th century. It is surprising how much inspiration and new ideas one can sometimes find even in the strangest of places.

"It turned out that, in the end, once streamlined, the process was quite simple. It really had to do with duplicating certain natural conditions that existed during the creation of the universe, with the most demanding precision. The secret was in creating an exact duplication of these conditions. You saw with your own eyes today that, beyond that requirement, not a huge amount of equipment is necessary.

"My people were thrilled when they learned I had at last succeeded in synthesizing stellite. Soon, factories were set up, and in a short amount of time, the first ships were ready to go out and explore the universe."

"I never heard of such ships," I said, not quite able to grasp in my mind the scope of what he was telling me.

"No, you wouldn't have. It happened... a long time ago," he said wistfully.

·I waited for more, but obviously he did not wish to elaborate.

"But if you... your people... had such ships, why are you now synthesizing stellite in your hangar, Doctor?"

He sighed very deeply, and his gaze, ordinarily so penetrating, took on a veiled, haunted look while his eyes fixated upon something unseen over my shoulder.

"My people and I... became estranged, Borel," he said. "I left of my own choice, and I've never regretted my decision. Still, except for my granddaughter, I'm now alone. As to having my own ship, yes, I, er, borrowed one," he continued after a brief hesitation, "but the ships made by my people carry a.... signature... within them..."

"A signature?"

"Something that is part of their design. For example, anyone among your military experts could immediately spot the difference between steel forged by Krupp and that coming from your own Le Creusot. Well, the same is true for our ships.

"So, since I came here, I've been trying to make my own ship. But the key to that is the ability to synthesize my own supply of stellite, which as you saw last night, is not an easy task. I've been very lucky until now, but that accidental explosion almost destroyed all my efforts. Fred can tell you that I was so angry at first, that I almost abandoned the whole enterprise.

"But then, I decided to go out for my morning stroll. During it, I realized that I could just as well finish the job in the secondary laboratory, which you saw. Clearly, I could never have synthesized the quantity of stellite I required in there, and the loss of my main laboratory remains a heavy blow. Fortunately, I'm now very close to my goal. I only had to make a few more thin layers of stellite to be finished. What you saw last night was all I needed before moving on to the next step. In fact, I even made a little extra. Look!"

And so saying, he pulled something that looked like a big, silvery-blue marble from his pocket.

He extended his hand as if to deposit it on a surface that was not there, and let it drop. It just hung there, in mid-air, as if suspended on an invisible string.

I looked at the amazing thing with awe when, suddenly, it emitted a low hum and vanished. I turned towards Doctor Omega, but he just smiled.

"Don't worry. Remember what I told you, it's not bound by the physical laws of our space."

Indeed, the blue marble reappeared, just as an object which is hidden by the shadow of a cloud becomes visible when the cloud passes and it is again bathed in sunlight.

I timidly reached out my hand to touch the marble.

"Go ahead," said the Doctor. "It's perfectly harmless in that state."

I took the stellite in the cup of my hand. It felt cold, and I could feel that same faint vibration that I had detected before when I had touched the metal sheet in the Doctor's closet.

I took a closer look at it, marveling at its wonders, then finally gave it back to the Doctor, who pocketed it as if it had been an ordinary pebble and not a miracle beyond nature.

"So you think that you can build a ship of that metal?" I said.

"More than merely think, young man. You've seen for yourself the sheets of stellite that I've manufactured, eh? You've even handled one yourself..."

I nodded.

"I've designed a basic prototype. Now she only needs to be cast, assembled and then plated with stellite to become operational and taken on her maiden journey– I'm planning to take her to your neighboring planet, Mars!"

I could not repress a surprised cough when I heard that. Mars! The fourth planet of our solar system! Like a new Columbus, this man was conceiving an expedition to another world!

"Mars! But, Doctor, it's... millions of kilometers away..."

"Fifty-six million kilometers at this time of the year because it's in perihelic opposition to Earth. But remember, Borel, distances no longer matter to us, because we won't be travelling in normal space. In fact, we won't be travelling just in space but in time as well."

"In *time*?"

"Yes. In order to test my craft properly, I need to see if it can move through other dimensions, not unlike those imagined by your Monsieur de Maupassant. Besides, Mars now is just an arid, dying world. Don't you want to see it as it was billions of years ago, when liquid water freely flowed on its surface, Borel?"

My mind reeled at the concepts this amazing old man was rattling out just as easily as an ordinary man might read from the Baedeker when planning a trip to Italy.

"I must tell you, Doctor... I'm deeply honored... I feel enormously privileged that you have chosen me to accompany you on such a momentous journey."

"Don't mention it, young man. You made an excellent impression on me the first time I set eyes on you."

"Can I ask you another question, Doctor?"

"Certainly."

"You mentioned that you had designed a prototype? She is not yet built then?"

"No, indeed, she's not. But I have entered into a correspondence with Monsieur Eugène Schneider. I sent him very detailed blueprints, and his factory in Le Creusot is presently executing my design."

"That must cost a fortune, Doctor."

"I am not without resources, young man. Would you like to see my plans?"

"Of course I would! It would be an honor."

"Then, come back with me to my laboratory. I'll be delighted to show you everything."

After giving Marcel some additional instructions, and telling him not to wait for me for dinner, I set out with Doctor Omega and Fred back towards the hangar.

Once there, we settled comfortably in the Doctor's study. It was a wood-paneled room, lined with bookshelves filled to the brim with books of all sizes and languages. There were also maps, some flat, others rolled in tubes, several astrolabes, a blackboard covered with equations, and hanging on a wall, a small painting of a beautiful woman that may have been a Fragonard, but I could not be certain.

The Doctor cleared the table and started unrolling several blueprints, showing various cut-aways of a projectile-shaped vehicle.

"But it looks like a cannon shell, Doctor!" I exclaimed. "Just like in Jules Verne's novel!"

The Doctor frowned and threw me a stern look.

"Be serious, young man. You can't compare my project to an imaginary voyage. Monsieur Verne's conception of space travel is entirely uñpractical, as you well know, while mine..."

"I'm sorry, Doctor," I quickly apologized.

"Harrumph. Unlike Monsieur Verne's fanciful cannonball, my own ship will be thirteen meters long, and three meters in diameter. The scientists of my... country... have developed techniques to make stellite shift its shape to accommodate the relative dimensions of their crafts..."

"Shift its shape? But how?"

"They use machines smaller than the eye... But do not concern yourself with that, Borel. I do not have the equipment here capable of manufacturing such wonderful devices, so by necessity our craft shall have to rely on more conventional means of dealing with the Martian topography, which is why I designed it to be both an underwater and an all-terrain vehicle."

My eyes grew wide in amazement at this man's genius.

"Yes, I said underwater and all-terrain. For we may have to cross polar seas and travel across rocky plains before we can reach the inhabited regions at the equatorial sector of the planet."

"So you believe Mars to be inhabited?"

"I'm reasonably certain of it, young man... But let's return to my blueprints. As you can see, the entire outside surface of the ship will be covered with removable sheets of stellite five centimeters thick... Those are the ones you saw yesterday... The outer and inner hulls will be made of a light carbon steel whose composition I calculated very precisely to achieve maximum durability and flexibility...

"The interior of the craft," the Doctor continued, pointing at the schematics, "shall be comprised of six chambers, all lit by electricity generated by a dynamo and a two hundred-horsepower, eight-cylinder engine.

"The interior rests on a complex gyroscopic system which I designed in order to always remain stable, no matter what the position of our craft. These are also powered by electricity, with a back-up pneumatic power source.

"I've also allowed for portholes made of ultra-resistant quartz, plated with a thin layer of transparent stellite, which I was manufacturing yesterday when you arrived.

"As to the propulsion of our vehicle once we reach Mars, it will be achieved thanks to electric power again... Do you see this propeller here?"

"Yes."

"It's telescopic and fully retractable. It will be connected to our engine by a torque shaft made of the same steel as the inner hull. With this, I can safely steer our craft above or under water."

"Are these wheels, here?"

"Tracks, young man! Made of four road wheels and two support wheels with elastic lining, shock absorbers and driving sprockets located at the rear, locked to the tracks by a chain. The suspension has individual springs and all of the road wheels are equipped with brakes in the event that a track breaks or falls off.

"When we decide to convert our ship into an all-terrain vehicle, I just need to push on that lever, and the chassis you see here in red will drop down by a full meter and fit in that space there just beneath the engines. It will be locked into place by those steel rods.

"That portion of the hull will slide out, and the tracks will be lowered onto the ground. I can pilot the vehicle from the bridge thanks to this steering mechanism I designed. I expect we'll achieve a cruising speed of about twenty-five kilometers per hour if the terrain is not too difficult."

"Ah, all this is wonderfully designed!" I said. "Doctor, you're a genius! An inventor that France will be proud to call her son in a few months when we return covered with glory!"

The Doctor did not respond to my patriotic fervor, and I thought I detected a look of evasion in his eyes, but could not fathom his meaning. Perhaps this great scientist did not trust his adopted country to treat him fairly? Or maybe he wasn't as confident as he sounded in our ability to return to our world alive and well?

"This, here," he continued after a small pause, pointing at another cut-away blueprint, "is how we'll be able to breathe during our journey. It's a device that employs electrolysis to make the oxygen we'll need..."

Then he pulled out one more cut-away that showed the craft in a vertical position and in its entirety, and not just the engineering sections. I could see that the ship was split into three levels, with a central column and a narrow spiral staircase in its center.

The top floor was clearly the bridge, where we would sit during the journey, and from which Doctor Omega would pilot his amazing vehicle.

The middle floor was divided into three rooms, each connected to the central column by a small door. Each room was furnished with a small, square wall cupboard, a bed, and a folding table attached to the walls.

The lower floor was divided into two rooms, one that led to the engines, and the other a store room where the Doctor, with foresight, had planned to keep food supplies, such as salted meats, preserves, biscuits, bottled water and ale.

While I studied these blueprints carefully, the Doctor was looking at me, gauging my reactions. Finally, I said:

"This is... amazing! Incredible! I can't wait to see the craft!"

"As I told you, the Schneider mills in Le Creusot have already begun manufacturing its component parts, young man. I received a telegram from Monsieur

Schneider himself last week. We shall be ready to take delivery of it in just under three months!"

During the next seven weeks, Doctor Omega and I spent much time together planning our journey. I helped Fred order and organize the supplies we would need, and assisted the Doctor with minor engineering revisions, taking down his hastily scribbled notes, and recopying them legibly in his logbooks.

Finally, the time came when we received a cable from Le Creusot, and the Doctor and I left for that great temple of French metallurgy.

When we reached the foundries, the massive craft had already been cast, but since she could not be made of a single piece, she had been divided into three sections, which had now to be bolted and welded together.

The Doctor examined the ship closely and declared himself satisfied with the metal work. During his long conversations with the engineers, I could see that most of them thought he was a rich eccentric, if not downright crazy, and that they had to humor him because Monsieur Schneider had ordered it.

I pondered over what mysterious leverage, other than money, the Doctor could have used on someone as powerful as Eugène Schneider, undoubtedly one of the wealthiest men in the country, in order to so bend him to his will. I suspected some kind of state secret which the old man had been understandably reluctant to reveal, and I respected his secrecy.

In any event, even if the engineers thought the Doctor was mad, they quickly came to respect his knowledge, and followed his instructions to the letter.

We spent another six, long, boring weeks in Le Creusot, during which time a crew of thirty workers labored hard to finish the ship.

Then, she had to be wrapped in a tarpaulin, and secured to a railcar, so that she could be transported by rail to Marbeuf, where the Doctor had cabled Fred instructions to have a new hangar erected to perform the last and most delicate task of all: applying the stellite plating to the craft's outer hull.

I shall spare you the thoroughly banal story of the return train journey from Le Creusot to Marbeuf, and how we had to hire a chariot pulled by no less than twelve strong Percheron horses in order to transport the ship from the station to the Doctor's new facility.

Upon our return, we were welcomed by the villagers, and I derived great satisfaction in sleeping in my own bed again.

I could at last enjoy Marcel's ministrations, and the pleasures of hearty Normandy cooking, which I had sorely missed in Le Creusot.

However, I had little time to relax, for work had to begin again in earnest.

With the help of Fred, and several local peasants who had been sworn to secrecy and paid off with a casket of good Bordeaux wine, the ship had been moved into the new hangar that was, to tell the truth, nothing more than a roof and four, quickly erected walls.

The job of plating the ship proved far trickier than we had realized. The stellite weighed literally nothing and had a disturbing tendency to float away if we let go, and even occasionally vanish from under our fingers.

The Doctor had provided Fred and I with a tool not unlike that strange screwdriver I had seen the big man use on the broken trionic lock, which performed the job of a welding tool.

We quickly learned to master it, and the job soon proceeded apace satisfactorily.

In a matter of days, all of the stellite plates had been affixed to the ship. Probably out of concern for the secrecy of his invention, the Doctor had insisted that the metal sheets be welded in a way that would make their removal possible if so desired. That, as we shall see, was to become crucial at a later date.

At long last, we were ready to embark upon our journey towards the heavens.

Chapter Three
The Cosmos *Takes Off*

Our ship was now ready for take-off.

With the help of pulleys and cables, it was erected inside Doctor Omega's new hangar, the roof of which had been removed for the occasion.

The Doctor had spent the last few days closeted in his study, performing arcane calculations in his note-book, or writing equations on his blackboard.

"Are you concerned that you may have made a mistake?" I inquired.

"Not in the least, young man," he replied. "But the most delicate task of all still remains to be performed. Without that outer shell of stellite, my new craft could not travel outside the four dimensions. But that is not enough. We need a steering mechanism.

"So, I've adapted a guidance system from my old ship. But if my calculations are wrong, we risk drifting aimlessly outside the continuum. That's why I keep rechecking my figures, you see?"

I shuddered at the thought of being condemned to float outside of space and time for all eternity, like the Flying Dutchman of legend. But the Doctor, ever the pragmatic one, reassured me that we would run out of air long before we reached the end of eternity!

Little did I know how prophetic his comment would turn out to be!

The next day, the Doctor locked himself in his laboratory, and spent several hours performing some mysterious tasks.

When he came out, he carried with him two devices which he later identified as a *temporal rotor* and a *vector generator*. To me, they looked like those convoluted African sculptures I had seen at the Paris World Fair, except that they were made of metal and glass instead of equatorial wood, or at least something that looked like metal and glass.

At the Doctor's request, I accompanied him to the bridge of our new ship. There, he asked me to hold on to the two devices, while he crawled on the floor under the steering wheel.

I soon heard the buzz of that strange screwdriver of his, and a few seconds later, he gestured to me to pass him the *temporal rotor* (which is how I learned its name), then the *vector generator*.

The moment he finished installing the two machines, I noticed that the entire craft came to life. I cannot find other words to describe it. It was the oddest of feelings.

One minute, we stood inside an inanimate metal hulk, no different from the French battleships I had once visited in the harbor of Brest; the next, we were inside a ship that vibrated in tune with what I thought were the harmonics of the universe itself.

I imagined that if one of Jonathan Swift's fabled Lilliputians could have stood inside my Stradivarius while it was being played by the great Paganini, he would have felt just as I did now.

It certainly was a wonderful sensation.

"Well, well," said the Doctor getting up, rubbing his hands and looking pleased with himself. He obviously had anticipated the phenomenon, and considered it a proof of his success.

"If only my colleagues from the Academy could see this," he muttered.

Then, he placed his hand on my arm in a fatherly gesture.

"You're lucky, Borel. You're going to become part of history. And not just of French history, eh?"

I was about to ask him what he meant by this when Fred walked in to tell us that the final supplies had just been loaded into the store room.

"I must ask you again, Fred," said the scientist. "Do you still want to come with us? The trip could be more dangerous than you think. Wouldn't you prefer to stay behind?"

The big man became indignant.

"Doctor! How can you say that? When you and Mademoiselle Susanne pulled me from that hell hole in Cayenne, I told you that I would never be able to repay your generosity. Now I can, and I will. Don't even think of leaving without me. I'll sleep aboard if it comes to that!"

The Doctor could not hide his pride at the fierce loyalty shown by his assistant.

"Besides, who's going to cook for you while you're on board? This gentleman from Paris? Ha! I wouldn't trust him near one of my skillets if my life depended on it!"

"He's right, Doctor. I'm a terrible cook," I said.

"And what if you're attacked by savages from the Moon? We don't know what kind of creatures live up there..."

"We're not going to the Moon, Fred," said the Doctor, smiling. "We're going to Mars. As far as the cosmos goes, it's a very different place."

"The Moon, Mars, the cosmos, it's all the same to me, Doctor. What if you're attacked by the marsupials?"

"They're called Martians."

"Martians, then. Do you think the two of you can defend yourselves against them? Not a chance! With me, at least you've got a chance. I'm very strong. That's why I'm coming, and that's all there is to it!"

Looking at Fred's huge hands and his broad shoulders; I agreed with him and was delighted that he was indeed coming. I had no fighting experience at all, and did not doubt that his experience would be essential during our journey.

"Thank you, Fred. I couldn't ask for a better friend," said the Doctor, shaking the big man's hand.

"We'll say no more of it then."

The day of our departure had been fixed by Doctor Omega for the morning of the following day: April 18th, 1905. A Tuesday.

The night before, morbid thoughts again preyed on my mind. I wondered whether this might be the last night of my life I would spend on God's Earth. I began questioning the wisdom of my going with the Doctor on his journey as my resolve weakened.

I turned over in my bed, and ceaselessly argued with myself.

At one point, I almost got up to tell the Doctor that I had changed my mind and decided to stay home after all, but I felt too ashamed to go through with that cowardly last minute gesture.

In the morning, I got up, took my bath, and dressed in my best country clothes, as if I was going hunting.

The time had come to take my leave of the world on which I had been born to embrace the heavens.

As I reached the hollow, I could see the craft shining softly in the morning light. A small crowd of villagers had already gathered around it.

The Doctor was pacing, rechecking some final calculations, writing in what looked like a pocket diary. Once in a while, he would raise his eyes to the sky, as if he could see Mars, or beyond, from where he stood.

"Perfect," he finally said to himself, pocketing the notebook.

He then walked to a small platform that had been erected at the foot of the ship to make access to its circular entrance easier.

Fred and I joined him.

The crowd had now grown to about fifty folks, including my own Marcel and Pierre, who had insisted on accompanying me so far.

I was pleasantly surprised when a few of the villagers pulled out some musical instruments and began playing a few bars from *La Marseillaise*.

"What are they doing that for?" asked the Doctor.

"Why, Doctor, it is played in the honor of men who put their lives at risk in the service of *la belle France*," I explained, genuinely moved.

"Harrumph."

"What's her name?" shouted someone in the crowd.

"What?"

"What's the ship's name? What is she called?"

"He's right, Doctor," I said. "You haven't baptized our craft."

The old scientist looked taken aback as if such a notion had never occurred to him.

"How about the *Cosmos*, Doctor?" suggested Fred.

"Yes, the *Cosmos*! That's a good idea!" I added.

"Well then, the *Cosmos* it is," said the Doctor, smiling.

"*Vive le Cosmos! Vive le Cosmos!*" shouted the crowd.

The Doctor looked at his watch.

"The time has come, I think," he said.

"*Alea jacta est*," I thought.

My heart was thumping furiously in my chest. I must have looked very pale. I might as well admit it here: I was very frightened.

The Doctor activated a hidden lock (which I hoped would work better than the one on his hangar), and the round door slid away, revealing the ship's narrow, central shaft.

Fred went in first... I was supposed to follow.

But I hung desperately to those last few minutes of fresh air and Normandy blue sky, filled with so much vibrant life.

I pretended to wave at Marcel and Pierre, like a man who said he would kill himself at noon on the dot waits for all the clocks of the city to toll their last before firing the fatal bullet.

"I'm waiting, Borel," said the Doctor testily.

For a fleeting moment, I thought of turning and running away, but I met the scientist's eyes, those penetrating, timeless eyes that had so transfixed me before, and again I became helpless before them.

I stepped into the craft, immediately followed by Doctor Omega.

The sound of the crowd cheering was abruptly cut off to barely a low mumble as the Doctor shut the door behind us and locked it.

We quickly climbed up to the bridge, where Fred had already harnessed himself in a chair to the Doctor's right.

I took the chair to the left, while the Doctor sat in the pilot's chair.

We were inclined at almost ninety degrees, parallel to the ship's axis. In front of me, and to my left and right, I could see perfect blue sky through the front and side portholes.

I looked at Doctor Omega. He seemed very calm and sure of himself, like a King reclaiming a throne to which he was born. An odd idea crossed my mind. This, I thought, was not the face of a man leaving, but of a man going home...

I also looked at Fred, who seemed happy and cheerful, and not in the least worried.

With a single flick of a switch, the Doctor activated one of the mysterious devices he had installed under the steering column, and a weird whistling sound filled the cabin, like that of an arrow wheezing past one's ear.

"It's a success! We've gone," said the scientist.

The blue sky outside had suddenly disappeared, and the bridge was now lit only by the cold glare of the electric lights.

Through the portholes, I could see a field of stars and, to starboard, what could only be–Earth!

We were the first men in the entire history of mankind to view our world thus, from space. It floated like a magical blue balloon, streaked with white clouds, against the velvety blackness of airless space.

I could make out the contours of the continents: the Americas stretching from pole to pole, Dark Africa, and the Asiatic land mass...

I could hardly repress my excitement.

"Earth! This is Earth! This is our world!"

Fred was also looking at that incredible sight, not believing his eyes.

I had seen that look at the *Musée Grévin* during some of the more amazing tricks performed by its prestidigitators. Was this but a fantastic illusion as well?

But in our hearts and minds, we knew it was no such thing. This was real.

In spite of the thickness of the hull and the electric heating, we began feeling the infinite coldness of space seep in through the shell of our vehicle.

Fred went down to the supply room, and quickly returned with fur-lined jackets, which were very welcome.

"What now, Doctor?" I asked.

"We're in orbit. The first step of our journey has been a success. But the greatest step remains to be taken. We're still in normal space. We must now leave this continuum."

"Couldn't we have done it from the surface?"

"In my old ship, yes, Borel. But this is only a prototype. It's as clumsy and primitive as a Roman galley would be when compared to one of your transatlantic liners...

"There are factors to be considered, such as the rotation of the planet, of the stars... Without the help of advanced calculating machines that you don't have, I couldn't take the risk. It was safer to use the stellite to propel us first to outer space before making the big jump... Are you ready, gentlemen?"

Both Fred and I nodded in concert.

The Doctor pushed another switch.

Suddenly, there was a loud moaning sound, and I felt as if we were falling.

At the World's Fair, I had amused myself on the *montagnes russes*, and remembered the sensation of plunging forward as the little chariots rolled down their mechanical slopes. It was the same feeling here, except that it seemed like we would never hit bottom.

Then, abruptly, it stopped.

Now, we felt as if we were entirely motionless, perfectly standing still. Yet, a quick look through the portholes quickly dispelled that illusion.

The stars had not gone, but they were now rotating around us, twirling around clouds of light and nebulae made of ever-changing colored matter. We were in a kaleidoscopic tunnel made of pure aether, cutting through the celestial fabric of the universe like a knife through butter.

Not for the first time, I admired the genius of Doctor Omega, and of his mysterious people, who had learned to navigate the ultimate sea that surrounded all of God's creation, like the Wright Brothers had liberated us from the gravity that tied us to the ground.

The Doctor got up to stretch his legs, and we did the same.

I stepped closer to the stellite-plated porthole and totally lost myself in the contemplation of the vortex-like patterns that gyrated outside the ship.

I did not even hear the Doctor appear behind me.

"Exhilarating, isn't it, Borel? Once you've walked in eternity, you can no longer be the same man as you were before, no more than a sailor or an aviator would," he said, again divining the nature of the emotions that filled my soul.

For once, I was speechless, and just nodded in complete agreement.

Suddenly, the Doctor leaned forward, and brought his face very close to the glass.

I looked in the direction he was looking, and noticed a very small point of light, at first no bigger than a pinhead, but which appeared to grow larger with every passing moment.

Quickly, it became a bluish, phosphorescent ball that seemed to be headed right at us.

"What is it, Doctor?" I asked.

"I don't know yet," he replied testily.

He continued to peer at the incoming phenomenon with growing concern. I was standing right behind him, also looking at the ball of blue fire that had now grown to the size of a balloon.

Suddenly, the Doctor turned around, his face an expression in shock and surprise.

"What is it?" I exclaimed.

"A helix, Borel! A very nasty thing! That fireball is one of the most dangerous things that exist outside the continuum. It's attracted to us like St. Elmo's fire is attracted to the mast of a ship during a storm. It's rushing straight at us. We can't avoid it!"

Fred and I looked at each other.

"Do you mean?..." I asked.

"Yes. When it hits us, we'll be completely annihilated! We'll become a scattering of atoms randomly spread throughout creation."

Then, aware of the responsibility he had shouldered when he had asked us to join him on this experimental journey, he added:

"My poor friends... I am so very sorry..."

If any of my readers ever have the misfortune of finding themselves on a sinking ship, they will recognize the fear one feels when being told to rush to the lifeboats and prepare to evacuate the vessel. It is a deep abiding fear, barely relieved by the sight of the tiny boats to which one will entrust one's life on the hostile ocean.

How much more terrifying was our situation, for we were in a ship lost on a sea that no humans had ever navigated, with no lifeboats to give us that momentary sense of having narrowly escaped death.

Our death was coming right at us. We saw it approach at astonishing speed, and there was nothing we could do to avoid it...

The *Cosmos* was doomed!

I doubt that there was ever a more awful and horrible experience. As I write these lines, I cannot recall those tragic minutes without a deep shudder.

Our initial panic gave way to resignation, and Fred and I began praying.

We fell to our knees and muttered barely remembered childhood prayers, recommending our souls to our Lord and Savior.

Doctor Omega, however, had not given up. He was pacing fiercely, his face creased in frustrated concentration.

"There must be something I can do... Something... Ah, if only I had my own..."

Suddenly, he stopped and his face beamed.

"Yes, of course!"

He rushed behind the pilot seat, and put his hands squarely on the switches; his entire body tensed, like a coiled spring.

"It must be exactly..."

The helix was now almost as big as a hot air balloon.

It was rushing towards us at terrifying speed. It had become so blinding that my unfortunate companions were no more than silhouettes in the light.

It was about to hit us when...

"...Now!" shouted the Doctor.

I heard him flick a switch, and the ship shook and groaned as the helix passed *through* us, harmlessly, like a ghost.

For a brief moment, everything was bathed in an almost pure white light, and I experienced the strange illusion that our craft had flattened. My sense of depth disappeared and it was as if we were characters drawn on a sheet of paper.

I screamed and nearly fainted. Fred fell to the floor like an ox.

Fortunately, all this was merely an illusion, and in the blink of an eye, the *Cosmos* returned to normal.

The Doctor's voice rang triumphantly in my ears, loud as a fanfare.

"We're saved, my friends! We're saved!"

I could hardly bring myself to believe it. I rubbed my eyes like a man emerging from a nightmare, and learned against the wall to catch my breath.

Then, I took a tentative look through one of the portholes.

I could still see the helix, but the fireball was now moving farther and farther away from us, until it was merely a bluish spark that eventually vanished from sight.

The Doctor was right. We'd been saved. Instead of crushing us, the helix had passed through us without harming us. But how could such a miracle have happened?

I looked at Doctor Omega with awe.

He was the one who had rescued us from that dire peril. I became further convinced that we had nothing to fear.

"Don't look so glum now," the scientist chided us. "I've never seen such long faces. You should be celebrating."

"We're definitely out of danger?" asked Fred.

"From the helix, yes," the Doctor responded, categorically.

"What exactly happened?" I asked. "For a minute, I experienced the strangest of sensations. It was as if everything had flattened..."

"Merely a sensory illusion, young man. The human brain finds it difficult to cope with multidimensional engineering.

"What I did was increase the number of our dimensions in space, so relatively we became larger than the helix, and it went through us like a pea through a giant hole.

"Of course, we couldn't sustain such a transition for more than the briefest of moments, not in this ship. So I had to wait for the very last minute before I could act. If I had been a second too early, or too late..."

"Is the ship all right?"

"Absolutely. We haven't even deviated from our course. Maybe our outer hull may have been lightly singed, but that's all."

"Congratulations, Doctor! I understood nothing about your explanations, but you've made a believer out of me. The *Cosmos* could be in no safer hands!"

"That goes for me too," said Fred. "But I still hope we don't encounter another one of those nasty helixes. I'll be happy to set foot on solid earth again."

"That may be difficult since we're going to Mars," I joked.

"Mars! Earth! The Moon! As long as there's dirt under my feet, it's all the same to me."

"I'll do my best, Fred," said Doctor Omega.

"Thank you, Doctor! And to show you my gratitude, I'm now going to prepare our lunch. How about a ham omelet?"

We both agreed that was a perfect choice, and the big man went down to the supply room.

Soon, I heard the familiar clanking noise of cooking utensils being readied, dishes being moved, and even if I was not mistaken, a bottle being popped open.

Meanwhile, the Doctor was absorbed with writing in his diary.

Occasionally, he shared an observation or a comment with me, which I dutifully put down in a big log book that I had brought aboard. But the truth was that he gave me very little to write.

I felt that he needed not as much a secretary on this journey as a man of like mind with whom he could share his adventures.

Without experiencing a sense of speed or even of movement, it was impossible to tell that we were in fact travelling in that strange tunnel that existed outside of normal space. I felt no bumps in our journey, only and very rarely a barely noticeable oscillation.

Outside the ship, there was only the twirl of the aether and the kaleidoscope of the heavens around us. Since our encounter with the helix, I no longer looked at this view with wonder, but with fear. I knew that this was a sea perilous beyond all the seas of Earth.

And, as with a sea voyage, the view was quickly becoming monotonous.

I would not recommend outer space to tourists who love picturesque locations and enchanting views. This was far too tiresome an experience.

"How much time is the rest of the trip going to take?" I asked the Doctor.

"Another eight hours or so," he replied.

"Ah!" I said with a grimace.

I was about to ask another question when, suddenly, we heard the sound of a muffled explosion coming from below. Almost immediately, I began to smell something burning.

We jumped to our feet and hurried down the stairs to the store room.

Fred, his face ruddy and congested, his eyes rolling, was trying to put out a fire that was threatening to consume the burner on which he was preparing to cook his omelet.

"Fire! Fire!" he screamed, using a dish towel to stop the fire from spreading to other parts of his improvised kitchen.

I rushed to grab a jar of water, but the Doctor stopped me with a gesture.

"No water, Borel! Use salt instead."

By chance, Fred had insisted on taking with us a fairly hefty barrel of sea salt, perhaps remembering that salt had once been a precious commodity with savages, and maybe intending to barter with hypothetical Martians...

Following Doctor Omega's advice, I started spraying salt liberally on and around the burner, smothering the blaze under a rain of white powder.

Meanwhile, the scientist was using another rag to help Fred put the fire out.

In a few minutes, we had it under control, then out altogether.

"What did you do, Fred?" I said accusingly.

"Nothing, M'sieur Borel, I swear," the big man replied, almost in tears. "I lit up the burner as I've done a million times before, and it just blew up in my face. It's a miracle I wasn't more badly burned..."

The Doctor sniffed delicately around the charred burner.

"Fred's right. The fire was not his fault. I should have guessed that something like this might happen..."

"What do you mean?" I asked.

"The helix went through our ship without causing any *visible* damage, but if my suspicions are correct, it altered the chemical properties of the petrol inside that burner. It made it far more volatile, either by accident... or design."

"By design? Do you mean to say that that fireball was... alive? That it intended to hurt us?"

"Perhaps it did, Borel. Perhaps it did... But that is not the most serious of the concerns now facing us right..."

"You're scaring me, Doctor. What is?"

"The lack of air. That blaze consumed more oxygen than can be replaced by my electrolysis machine during the time we've left..."

I saw the Doctor's face crease in worried concentration.

"We may run out of air before we reach Mars. Ah, it's too stupid!"

"I'm sorry, Doctor," said Fred. "I just wanted to cook you a good omelet. I'd never guess that that damned burner was sabotaged by that... that hellfire ball!"

"That's all right, Fred. As I said, you couldn't have known."

"Is there anything we can do, Doctor?" I asked.

"I think I have enough equipment and electrical power to build us an atmospheric revitalization device, but whether it will be enough, I don't know..."

"You can make new air?"

"After a fashion. First, the carbon dioxide we exhale will be filtered and accumulated in a container. Then it will be combined with hydrogen in a catalytic converter to produce methane gas and water. The methane will be vented outside the ship, and the water will be broken down into new oxygen for breathing and hydrogen for reuse in the process.

"While I make this, you two should lie down and sleep. We need to conserve as much oxygen as possible

78

and avoid any kind of physical effort. Even conversation."

"I don't know if I can sleep, Doctor..."

"You must, Borel, you must. There's no other choice."

We followed Doctor Omega's instructions and retired to our quarters.

Before lying down, I made some more notes in my log book. Now, re-reading them sixteen months later, I'm struck by their banality and even incoherence, a fact which I am inclined to attribute to oxygen deprivation.

At one point during the journey, the Doctor dropped by to tell me that, according to his calculations, we would reach Mars in time, but just barely.

I reflected that he seemed unaffected by our predicament, but went back to my fretful sleep before I had time to ponder this further.

The ship had become a torture chamber. Its atmosphere was heavy and literally almost impossible to breathe. I knew the end of our journey was close, but could not help wondering if the Doctor had made a mistake in his calculations. What if we landed too late? This ship could become our coffin.

I was beginning to suffocate. I tried to take in only small, measured breaths. But nothing helped.

I eagerly counted the minutes, waiting for the moment when we would be released from what had possibly become our ultimate prison.

I must have drifted into unconsciousness, for I was suddenly awakened by a loud moaning sound, followed by a thud.

Then I felt a breeze on my face!

Oh, the joy of fresh air! Taking a deep breath, filling one's lungs with precious, life-giving oxygen!

The door to my cabin was opened, and a gentle wind was blowing through the ship.

Doctor Omega stood there, smiling.

"We have landed on Mars," he said simply.

Chapter Four
Beneath the Sea of Ice

The *Cosmos* was floating gently upon the surface of the sea.

There was barely any wind in the air.

The water was a deep bottle green, almost dark, and very still, much calmer than any seas I had ever encountered on Earth. It looked like a vast icy mirror, reflecting the pale light of the sun from the zenith above.

The sun, much smaller than it appeared from our world, did not provide much warmth, but gave the scenery around us a near-crystalline quality that I had never seen before.

The ocean filled our entire horizon, as far as the eye could see. Here and there, chunks of ice lay motionless, embedded into the sea as if they had been dropped there by a celestial giant, like cherries into a cake.

Some were huge icebergs that loomed like towers in the distance.

Even at mid-day, the sky was of a remarkable pale rosy color, one evoking only the most beautiful of Earth's dawns, but without their underlying radiance.

The air was breathable, if biting cold. The ship's barometer showed nine hundred millibars of pressure.

Doctor Omega had told us that our craft had rematerialized in the Martian atmosphere before coming down slowly in the Northern Ocean, like a big, fat seagull preparing to land. In effect, it was as if we had landed in the Atlantic Ocean near Greenland on Earth.

At the Doctor's command, Fred had activated the ingenious mechanisms which rotated our rooms alongside the ship's axis, folded the furniture, and turned our craft from a projectile into a vehicle.

We were still required to crawl through the central shaft to move from one part of the ship to another, but at least we could stand up elsewhere.

Millions of questions rushed through my mind as we settled in our chairs back on the bridge.

The Doctor had informed us that this was Mars as it had existed more than three billion years ago. In our own time, the planet had become a desert. We had missed its beauty and its glory. It made me sad, and reminded me of Shelley's immortal poem: "*My name is Ozymandias, King of Kings, / Look upon my works ye Mighty, and despair! / Nothing beside remains. Round the decay / Of that colossal wreck, boundless and bare / The lone and level sands stretch far away.*"

Could the same fate someday be in store too for our own blue planet?

I shook off these morbid thoughts and concentrated on what the Doctor was doing.

He and Fred had finished checking that everything on board was in perfect working order. The electric engines were providing much welcomed heat, and our oxygen shortage was now a thing of the past.

"Gentlemen, we're going to begin our undersea exploration, while maintaining a southern course in order to reach land," said the Doctor.

He began to fill the ship's ballasts and, slowly, our craft sank.

Through the portholes, I saw a whirlpool of small bubbles rise, and little green waves of water flap around the ship.

But instead of sinking further down as I expected, the *Cosmos* suddenly remained still with us barely beneath the surface.

"We've stopped? Why?" I asked.

"I just want to be safe," said the Doctor. "I'm concerned that our stellite shell may have been somehow damaged or tampered with by the helix... But obviously I see that that hasn't happened. Our ship seems as seaworthy as it is spaceworthy... So we can now proceed!"

The *Cosmos* began sinking again.

Soon, the radiance of the surface vanished. From dark bottle green, the water became inky black.

The Doctor looked at its instruments, then unfolded the forward propeller. Under the power of our electrical engines, we began moving through the depths of the Martian sea.

"Everything is working admirably," said the Doctor. "I have to be prudent, because as you must have noticed by now, Martian gravity is only a third of Earth's. A two hundred-pound man like you, Fred, only weighs seventy-five pounds on Mars..."

Fred looked perfectly amazed at the revelation. He frowned and lifted his arm, looking at it as if it was somehow different!

"Thus it was not necessary to completely fill our ballasts to reach this depth level. We're now perfectly steady, and our hull is coping with the pressure very well. When we need air, we'll just have to resurface, but even with a stop or two, at this speed, I estimate we'll reach the closest land mass to the south in a day or so at most."

The scientist locked in a course, then relaxed in his chair.

We travelled thus for several interminably long hours.

A powerful electric lamp located at the prow of our ship projected a beam of light that was immediately swallowed up by the darkness.

To keep himself busy, Fred was unknotting some electric wires that he had taken with him, cutting them with pliers, and making them into spools.

I confess that I thought that our journey had become even more tiresome than before.

But then, suddenly, I began noticing that the sea around us was no longer filled with total darkness.

I could now see the vague outlines of fish swimming by, or perhaps it was some wild plant life from the bottom?

Sometimes, the glow became brighter, and at other times, it seemed to disappear almost completely.

I wondered what strange phenomenon could be the source of the mysterious luminosity?

Then, I quickly discovered the solution to this mystery.

The entire sea had suddenly begun to glow... It was like something out of a fairy-tale... An unforgettable sight...

I saw underwater trees with huge trunks, and red and yellow flowers, embellished with what seemed to be glittering pearls.

I saw a profusion of white cupolas, transparent as the purest of crystals, topped with pink crown-like membranes that palpitated gently as they glided along the sides of huge grottos made of giant sponges, slowly inhaling and exhaling in the deep.

These bizarre medusae seemed attracted to a large trench, a bottomless abyss leading to some unfathomable depths out of which came a shiny green mist.

As our craft drifted by, I saw bushes of needle-like vegetation with elaborate webs of luminous crystalline strands woven between their spiky leaves. They looked like upside-down chandeliers, sparkling and reflecting the fires of a thousand lights through their polished stones.

Our portholes had become giant kaleidoscopes through which all the glorious Martian sea life proudly displayed their wonders for our sole, privileged enjoyment.

Periodically, however, the darkness returned and obscured this delightful landscape.

A galaxy of a thousand points of lights vanished, before reforming and again illuminating this astonishing underwater scenery like a living rain of light.

"What can be the source of that light?" I asked the Doctor. "At this depth, it can't be the sun..."

"Look above, young man," he said.

I raised my eyes and saw strange, elongated fish with triangular heads swim rapidly past our ship.

I could not repress a movement of surprise, for I now understood that it was the natural phosphorescence emitted by those fish that illuminated our surrounding scenery!

"This is more fun than the tunnels of the *Métropolitain*," said Fred, whose eyes were like those of a child looking through the window of a toy store.

The number of phosphorescent fish around us kept increasing.

They were above us, below us; they surrounded us completely... Obviously, they were attracted to our ship, probably because of its own source of light...

Soon, we had to slow our progress, because we were now moving in the midst of a veritable school of these fish. I could even hear the crunching sound their bodies made against the outside metal of our craft.

I thought that I heard some distant screeching... A guttural, monotone shout, not unlike a far-away scream... But I blamed my overactive imagination...

This sea must be inhabited by some prodigious monsters, I thought. Gigantic prehistoric beasts, unlike any ever seen on Earth...

At one point, Fred pointed out to me some long, brown snake-like things that undulated and slithered rapidly among the undersea vegetation. One of these creatures swam closer to our ship, and I saw that it was hairy like a caterpillar, and bore an infinity of tiny but deadly-looking claws on its belly.

I also saw, floating lazily around us, some fat round fish, with a shape similar to that of a well-filled purse, except that their heads were crowned with a bushel of tentacles lashing incessantly around them.

I jumped back in horror as one of these tentacled monsters became attached to my porthole.

Suddenly, the *Cosmos* was brought to a violent stop, its entire frame shaking.

"We've run into something!" said the Doctor.

Indeed, our propeller had hit and become stuck into an as-yet unidentified obstacle. I thought it might be one of the sponge-like grottos we had seen before. At first, I could only see a greenish mass and some great curved white objects that looked like an umbrella frame.

The Doctor leaned forward towards the stellite-plated porthole to better study the artifact, then immediately shrank back in horror.

"It's a fish! We've rammed a fish!" he exclaimed.

"A f-fish?" I said, stuttering.

"More like a huge cetacean. Some kind of Martian orca that crossed our path. We've hit it in the chest. What you see are its flesh and bones."

As soon as he had finished explaining that gruesome truth, the *Cosmos* was shaken with extreme violence, and we were carried away at incredible speed.

The wounded creature was obviously trying to shake us loose, and was dragging us with it in its doomed flight.

The Doctor tried to pull and fold back the propeller without breaking it, for it was now the hook upon which the giant beast was entangled.

Meanwhile, the fish kept swimming in a straight line at great speed, then stopped and shook again, rendering any maneuvering impossible.

The Doctor shut off our engines in order to pose the least possible resistance, hoping that the creature would be successful in its efforts before it smashed us.

Slowly, the front of our ship began to slip out. But the fish then stopped moving, and we remained stuck.

"Perhaps it's dead?" I said.

"If we go in reverse, we might now be able to extricate ourselves," said the Doctor.

But as soon as the scientist again started the engines, the monster, who obviously was not dead, renewed its frenzied run.

I looked at Doctor Omega.

He was very pale, but sat firmly at the controls, looking for any opportunity to save us.

Fred and I were beginning to feel sick from all of the turning and shaking.

But the worst was yet to come.

Suddenly, with amazing speed, the creature began twisting upon itself at a mad pace...

We heard–and felt–numerous thumps upon the hull of the *Cosmos*.

We thought the end had come.

Then, we saw the entire sea light up brilliantly around us.

We beheld a horrible spectacle... What we had just felt was the death trashing of the creature, being eaten alive by thousands of phosphorescent fish who, like the piranha of the river Amazon on Earth, had been drawn by its blood!

They threw themselves onto the carcass which they devoured with grisly intensity.

I became suddenly violently sick, and had to rush to my quarters to throw up.

When I returned to the bridge, Doctor Omega had managed to pull us out of the creature. I could see from its bloody remains that it looked not unlike a killer whale, but with tentacles on both sides of its mouth.

The Doctor skillfully piloted our craft back to its earlier depth level, and we soon returned to our previous course.

Once again, our friend's calm composure and re-sourcefulness had extricated us from a dire peril, but I no longer felt totally reassured.

Fred, on the other hand, had become abnormally cheerful, likely a compensation for the fear he had felt during the attack.

He joked, laughed at anything, whether it was an odd-looking fish swimming past our portholes, or a bit of alien vegetation we encountered on our journey.

"Someday, I'll be back to do some serious fishing around here," he said. "In the Seine, I've got to wait an entire day before I catch anything. But here... look at all those fish!"

We had been travelling for several hours when I noticed that the waters around us had begun to change colors.

The sea was now a deep, dark red, yet still illumi-nated, even though the phosphorescent fish had long gone.

We tried to discover what could account for this new phenomenon, and eventually found that the reddish light came from huge, underwater, pyramid-shaped, rocks that were as transparent as crystal, and inside which shone bright columns of burning fire.

"They look like glass volcanoes," remarked Fred.

"Your description is more accurate than you think, my good Fred," said the Doctor. "They are indeed vol-canoes, fissures to the molten core of the planet spewing liquid quartz. Contact with the icy waters has solidified the crystalline lava and made these cones. But you can still see it spewing forth inside..."

"We've seen a lot of very strange things on this trip, haven't we, Doctor?" said Fred, shaking his head in wonder. "If I try to tell all this to my folks back home, for sure they'll think I'm crazy... Look over there! Just behind those glass volcanoes... It looks like houses!"

"Houses? At the bottom of the sea? You must be crazy, Fred!" I laughed.

Fred looked a little hurt by my derisive comment, but the big man was too good-natured to sulk. He kept peering at the underwater landscape, but could no longer find what he had seen.

Then, suddenly, we saw him jump backward and point his finger at the porthole.

In a strangled voice, he said:

"Doctor! M'sieur Borel! There's a man looking at us!"

We rushed to look.

There was indeed a man, or rather a man-like creature, with two legs, two arms, and a head, looking at us. But that is where the similarities stopped.

His skin was green and scaly all over. His face was clearly reptilian, with two enormous, round black or dark red eyes, with neither white nor pupil. His mouth was a dark gash. His nose was flattened to the point of non-existence, and instead of ears, I could see two reddish slits, not unlike gills, on the side of his head.

I shuddered while looking at him, for he reminded me of the sculptures of the devils I had seen on cathedrals.

He had gotten a grip on the outside of the ship with one hand, while with the other he held a barbed lance. I could see plates of armor on his body, and what I had taken to be the top of his skull was in fact a crude helmet made of some hard shell.

He looked like a terrifying, war-like figure, a demon from the icy depths.

He managed to hold on to our craft for a while, in spite of the turbulence created by the propeller. It was impossible to read his face, but he seemed hostile.

He angrily began to hit our ship with his clawed, webbed hand and his lance. I could hear the screams of the metal, and his sibilant hisses of rage.

Then, he crawled towards the circular door that was the entrance to our ship, using his webbed feet to cling to the hull.

He clawed and pulled at it, trying to open it by sheer force.

"We must do something, Doctor!" I shouted. "His strength seems prodigious. If he succeeds, we'll all drown!"

"And I can't even get out to punch him in his ugly face!" said Fred.

"Yes, we must do something," muttered the Doctor, obviously thinking hard. "But I didn't install any defensive systems..."

"What if we emptied the ballast? That would propel us back the surface?"

"And find ourselves stranded in the middle of the ocean? And then what, eh? We don't know how many of these... warriors... there are. They could surround us, prevent us from going forward or retreating... No, we must find another way."

Meanwhile, the noise from outside had increased. The underwater warrior was now using his lance to try to pry the door open. I thought I heard the metal buckle.

"Hurry up, Doctor, or we'll all be doomed!"

Doctor Omega did not answer me, but grabbed the electric wires Fred had been working on and rushed to the engine room.

Naturally, we followed him.

Once there, we saw him unroll some wire and connect them to the dynamo. The electric motors were humming.

Then, he carefully unscrewed a bolt to expose the outer metal of the hull beneath.

"Stay away from the walls," he told us.

He brought the live end of the wire in contact with the metal.

We heard a high-pitched shriek outside. The Doctor had succeeded in administering a powerful electric shock to our reptilian foe!

We looked through the nearest porthole, and saw the underwater warrior swim away at great speed in a haphazard pattern.

"I think you fried him good, Doctor," said Fred, shaking his head in contentment.

"I was hoping to not kill him, but I couldn't control the voltage, and I had no idea of how much current these creatures can tolerate, but he seemed very strong... I'm glad I didn't miscalculate..."

"Sometimes, you can't make an omelet without breaking some eggs," Fred noted.

"Let's hope he doesn't return with his friends," I said.

"We'd better get out of here fast then."

We were all in agreement with that last statement.

Back on the bridge, the Doctor increased our speed.

"This may seem odd, but I thought that this creature looked just like the Thalassites mentioned by Pliny the Elder," I remarked. "The description he gave of them is exactly like that underwater warrior. Is it possible that there may have been folks like him on Earth in our distant past?"

"Well, there are legends of mermaids and mermen, and of sunken Atlantis," said the Doctor pensively. "I suppose everything is possible. Some of the Earth-born underwater people may have become extinct, or they may still be around, hiding somewhere beyond the reach of humanity..."

"I'm sure they don't want to end up in a zoo," I said. "Any explorer would give an arm and a leg to bring back one of those. Think of the glory..."

The Doctor threw me a stern, disapproving look.

"Living creatures are not meant to be caged, Borel. Ever. Never forget it!"

Chastised, I nodded, and we continued on our journey.

The glass volcanoes, as Fred had nicknamed them, were now becoming more frequent. We obviously had entered a zone of great telluric activity.

We navigated nimbly, careful not to collide with one of them.

Sometimes, their bizarre shapes, due to the random congealing of the molten quartz, reminded me of giants made of crystal, who had found refuge in the depths but remained ready to pounces on an unwary traveller, like in the ancient myths.

Some of these volcanoes were very active and glowed a bright, crimson red. Others only shone a softer orange.

We had to navigate very cautiously for they reflected each other's images, creating *trompe l'oeil* illusions; they also projected the image of a distorted *Cosmos* back at us.

Around us, the water was bubbling naturally, and seemed sprinkled with small golden flecks.

Candidly, I have never seen a more impressive sight in my life, either before or after.

It looked like we had been transported to some fantasy Kingdom... To a land of dreams ruled by invisible spirits...

Then, the lights dimmed, and we went back to moving in a velvety kind of darkness; it was not total night, but a weird twilight.

A little later, we were entirely enveloped by a subtle, glowing mist.

Then, we began hearing a noise not unlike the roar of a waterfall. The water, which had been perfectly calm until now, began to grow agitated and churn around us.

The ship was thrown off course several times, and the Doctor was forced to keep a firm grip on the wheel to steady its progress.

The scientist peered ahead with a worried look on his face. In spite of its considerable weight, it was obvious that the *Cosmos* was but a toy to the forces ahead of us.

The situation seemed perilous again.

"We can't stay where we are," Doctor Omega finally decided. "These currents will tear the ship apart if we do. We'll have to dive deeper. Fred, help me fill the ballasts."

Fred hurried to assist the Doctor. He pushed several levers, and with a whistling sound, water rushed into our flanks, and the *Cosmos* began going down.

When the Doctor thought we had reached calmer waters, he ordered Fred to close the ballasts, and our course leveled off.

The reddish light was back. We soon came across more glass volcanoes, except that this time, instead of being craggy and randomly spread, they were perfectly straight, like huge posts sculpted out of crystal, and laid out in perfectly aligned patterns that went on as far as our eyes could see.

It looked like the alignments of megalithic stones that I had seen at Carnac in Brittany, but on a scale that defied human comprehension.

Indeed, I was sure that no men had built that gargantuan display.

As we entered this prodigious alley, we noticed that the landscape around us had also changed.

Gone was the wild and savage nature that we had seen on the ocean floor before.

Instead, great spongy trees and gigantic algae forests rose beneath us; they looked ordered, symmetrical, like plantations instead of a natural jungle.

I could even see the patterns of roads or paths criss-crossing them; they met in large, perfectly circular rings cut out of the vegetation.

I knew that this was no caprice of nature, and what I was looking at was the mark of a powerful civilization.

The more we progressed, silently gliding in the waters above the amazing landscape, the more astounded we all became.

Suddenly, we came across what I cannot call anything but a city. It was made up of squarish shapes all conglomerated together in a way that reminded me of a beehive.

"Down there! That's the same kind of house I saw earlier," shouted Fred.

We then realized that Fred had been right, and what he had seen before may have been an outpost of the strange civilization that thrived beneath us.

"If those are same kind of houses, then I guess that..." I said, without daring to complete my sentence.

The Doctor grabbed a spyglass and looked down through a porthole.

"Your guess is indeed correct, young man. Look," he said, handing me his instrument.

I brought it up to my eyes and looked below.

What I saw froze me with horror.

Hundreds, maybe a thousand, of reptilian warriors thronged beneath us, swimming in and out of their rugged houses!

I had seen crowds congregate at major sporting events, or mill about a market, but this was not the spectacle I beheld now. This was a disciplined throng, like an army preparing for war.

I had a sinking feeling in the pit of my stomach.

As if to prove me right, the *Cosmos* began to nose dive.

The portholes became suddenly obscured, as if a large blanket had been thrown over them.

"What does this mean? What's going on?" said Fred, rushing between observation windows.

"It's them, isn't it?" I asked the Doctor. "The underwater warriors."

"Yes, I think that's a safe assumption, Borel," the scientist replied. "They must have seen us approach. They're obviously very aggressive and xenophobic. I assume they have us trapped in some kind of net. They're trying to drag us down..."

Through the pale luminosity that still filtered from the outside, I could but barely discern their ghastly clawed, webbed hands tying ropes around our craft.

"Are we lost, this time?" I said. "Couldn't we shock them with electricity as you did before?"

"There are too many of them, I think," said the Doctor. "If we deplete our batteries, we'll die for certain."

Fred was hitting his head with his fist.

"By God and the Virgin Mary! Everything but that! I don't want to die at the hands of these monsters!"

"They probably don't realize it, but we'll drown or be crushed by the pressure if they succeed in opening our craft," remarked the Doctor.

He had not lost his *sang-froid*, and in fact, seemed to draw energy from these perilous situations. He became taller, more awe-inspiring. Doctor Omega was obviously one of these born leaders whose qualities of reason and purpose were never affected by the circumstances, no matter how dire.

"Earlier, young man, you suggested that we empty the ballasts and return to the surface, and I was the one who objected. But this time, I think you're right. We've no other alternative."

So saying, he pushed the levers that would pump the water out, and simultaneously engaged the electric motors into overdrive.

The *Cosmos* immediately shot up, nose first.

The propeller chewed the algae net and cables that tied us down like so many spider webs. And, in spite of our foes' intense resistance, we began our rapid ascension.

As we climbed up, we picked up even more speed. The hull groaned under the shifts in pressure, but we held fast.

The final strands of algae and webbing slipped off the craft. We could then take an unobstructed look through the portholes, and saw with enormous relief that we had left our enemies behind–or rather, beneath.

The Doctor wisely slowed down our rate of ascension to ease the pressure on the craft.

"We might as well use this opportunity to replenish our air," said the scientist.

A few minutes later, we emerged from the sea.

Doctor Omega had calculated our course so precisely that the *Cosmos* barely made a splash, and broke the surface of the water gently.

After unlocking the door, we all took in a deep breath.

The air had a vague smell of sulfur, but the Doctor explained that this was a result of its mixing with the excess carbon dioxide from within the ship. That phenomenon was of short duration, and soon we filled our lungs with good fresh air.

Our eyes were blinking as we tried to get re-accustomed to the light. We were like owls surprised by the dawn.

The dim light of the day seemed pallid by contrast with the magnificent spectacles we had beheld beneath the waters, but none of us were unhappy to have left those perilous waters.

We took a survey of where we were: once more, the sea was perfectly still, littered with ice floes, and massive icebergs that sparkled in the sun.

The Doctor used his spyglass to explore the horizon.

Suddenly, he let out a shout of joy and pointed in a direction.

"Land ahead! We've reached our destination!"

Neither Fred nor I could yet see any signs of land, but we knew we had finally crossed the Sea of Ice.

We were soon to set foot on a new continent, one that no human had ever trod before.

Chapter Five
The Red Hills of Mars

Doctor Omega did not hide his enthusiasm at the prospect of soon being able to explore a whole new world. His eyes shone like electrical bulbs, and his entire figure expressed his impatience to come across new, fascinating discoveries.

Do I dare admit that I did not share his feelings? After our previous encounters at the bottom of the sea of ice, I was far more apprehensive about what new perils might lie in wait for us.

I feared the strange new beings we might encounter on these Martian lands. Would they be as savage and hostile towards us as the underwater warriors had been? Or on the contrary, would they prove kind and benevolent?

Now that the horizon was becoming closer with every passing minute, I could see the land ahead, and it was anything but a welcoming sight. It looked like an icy slope littered with rocks, with reddish hills in the distance.

Suddenly, our ship hit bottom with an audible thud. We had reached shallow waters.

The Doctor stopped the engines. After pulling the propeller back, he released the locking mechanisms that had held our automotive tracks inside the hull beneath our feet. Fred supervised the delicate operation from below, and gave the Doctor precious directions, like the pilot of a Mississippi river boat.

I watched the slow transformation of our ship from a marine vehicle into a landbound one with enormous interest, again marveling at Doctor Omega's engineering ingenuity.

Eventually, the wheeled tracks were lowered onto the gravelly shallows beneath us and locked into place. The Doctor restarted the engines and they gripped the rocks with a grinding noise.

The *Cosmos* began to lumber forward towards the shore, like the mechanical Ironclads so well described by the astonishing Mr. H. G. Wells in one of his recent novels.

"Now let us stretch our legs a little," said the Doctor stopping the engines as we finally emerged out of the water.

The round door that was the entrance to our craft slid open, revealing a bleak landscape.

The *Cosmos* now rested on a desolate beach.

Before me, I saw an ancient landscape that had been ground down by millions of years of ice and erosion. The red hills stood to the east and south of us. Many intrusive rocks made of dark-red or black stones cut across the ground, rising from deep below and breaking through the sand like the claws of some mythical beast trapped underground.

Large pumpkin-sized boulders stood ahead of us, and I guessed that they would make the continuation of our journey difficult. I was reminded of Iceland, which was described by the great writer Pierre Loti as "*a somber country, sad and cold, full of stones, more stones, nothing but stones.*"

Fred was the first to jump down to the ground. His movements seemed odd, slower than usual, and his motion was like that of an inflatable balloon buffeted by the wind.

I suddenly remembered what the Doctor had told us about Martian gravity being one third of Earth's!

"It's funny. I'm walking like a bird," shouted Fred.

"Move more carefully," the scientist advised him. "Take smaller steps."

After a few minutes of practice, we all mastered the art of walking in lighter gravity. It was not unlike dancing, an art which I had practiced with some success in my youth.

The Doctor returned to the ship to fetch his spyglass. Myself, I grabbed a metal bar to use as an alpenstock from our supply room, while Fred took a big walking stick which he nonchalantly threw over his shoulder.

Thus equipped, we decided to embark on our first exploratory journey. We had decided to walk towards a small nearby hill from which the Doctor thought he would be in a better position to chart our future course.

We had travelled perhaps only a couple of kilometers when we heard a strange rustling sound, reminiscent of a low wind blowing through reeds.

Then, we heard yet another noise... It sounded like moaning... A sad, monotone wailing, like that of frogs in a swamp.

We looked at each other in surprise. We stopped and began looking warily around us.

"There!" said Fred, pointing to his right. "Martians!"

I shall never forget the horrible sight I next beheld.

A throng of dwarfish creatures was slowly advancing upon us. Their intentions, at that stage, remained unknown, but I could not help but shrink away in horror and loathing.

They were just under two feet high. Their big, bulbous, moon-like heads were out of proportion with their small bodies. Their eyes were round and red, and circled with dark green. They had no noses to speak of, and their thin lipless mouths made a disgusting chewing motion, like cows eating their cud. They looked abominably hungry.

The skin of their bodies was so pale that it was almost transparent. It was shiny as if oozing with a slimy veneer of fat. They were supported by stick-like legs that appeared to be jointed like a grasshopper's.

Their long, skeletal arms were extended in front of them, and ended with tentacle-like fingers which writhed and lashed while making a hideous suction noise.

Some of the gnomes were mounted on small creatures with long anteater-like noses and a skin similar to theirs. Their tentacles clutched the heads of their beasts, and because of the semi-transparence of their skin, I could see that they were feeding upon them.

As they marched forward, I noticed that they were the source of the noise we had heard earlier. They were like cicadas emitting their own, inhuman song.

"What are they, Doctor?" I asked.

Doctor Omega seemed neither frightened nor disgusted by the creatures, as Fred and I were. He observed them as a naturalist would a new species of bird that he had just catalogued, with a cold, scientific detachment that I envied.

"It's too early to tell, Borel," the scientist replied. "Wild creatures, certainly. Perhaps castaways from a more powerful civilization? You've seen the animals they're riding, eh? They draw nourishment from them. It must be very difficult to find food in this terrible climate. They've obviously developed some sort of parasitic relationship..."

"I don't know what you're talking about, Doctor," said Fred, "but I'm nobody's food."

"He's right, Doctor. They look to me like they want to add us to their menu."

The number of Martian dwarves had not stopped growing. Where they came from, I could not guess, but it looked like the ground itself was spawning them by the dozen.

"Hmm... Perhaps I can communicate with them..."

The Doctor tried speaking, in several languages, only a few of which I recognized. I saw him make universal gestures of salutation and peace, crossing his hands to his chest and bowing his head.

But none of that had any effect. In fact, the dwarves became even more aggressive.

Two of them jumped on the Doctor and grabbed his legs with their tentacles, while emitting some strident screeches.

The scientist let out a scream, as one of the monsters succeeded in biting his flesh under the thick cloth of his trousers.

Fred immediately hit the creature with his stick, while I, mastering my feelings of revulsion, pulled the other one off like one pulls a tick off a dog.

More Martians rushed to attack us. But Fred and I, he using his stick and me my alpenstock, were more than able to keep them at bay. Even the Doctor put his spyglass to good use by fending them off with it.

The dwarves were stronger than their frail appearance may have led us to believe. While Fred broke more than a few limbs and skulls, many of the creatures were somehow able to get up and attack again.

They came at us in waves, and we had the devil of a time repelling them. The crunch our weapons made when they hit their slimy bodies was truly nauseating.

They were obviously unused to encountering such fierce resistance, for after their first assault had been thrown back, they stopped coming at us and just stood there, observing us with their terrifying, hungry eyes.

"If all Martians are like that pack of rabid marmosets, we're in trouble," said Fred.

But the Doctor's face reflected only an intense scientific curiosity.

"I'm puzzled by their physiology," said the scientist. "Look at their heads. They're enormous. Their brains must be oversized. We should be confronting intelligent beings, highly evolved, instead of these mindless savages motivated only by their base instincts... Why is that, eh?"

"If you don't mind, Doctor," I said, "that's a question for another day. I suggest we beat a hasty retreat before more of those things crawl out of wherever they came from."

"Hmm? Yes. Yes, you're right, Borel. We should return to the ship. A pity though..."

We began retracing our steps, carefully, always keeping an eye on the Martians.

As we moved back, I could not help noticing that some of them, the bravest or maybe the hungriest, were slowly inching forward towards us again.

Fred and I gripped our weapons, ready to fight again if they got too close.

However, we did not have to.

Suddenly, a loud roar broke over the rocky plain. Then another, which sounded even closer.

Moved purely by instinct, we huddled closer to each other, as men must have done since the Stone Age when confronted by some unknown threat.

Without any further warning, yet another vision of horror appeared between the craggy boulders and sparkling rocks that surrounded us. It was a beast unlike any I had ever seen on Earth. A frightful, terrifying sight.

It was perhaps eight feet wide at the shoulder, with two long, pointy tusks that shone like deadly blades of steel on either side of its jaw, and two nasty-looking horns that curved forward on its head.

It had thick, coarse, grey hair, covering a bulky body that reminded me of the trigonocephalic mastodon that some paleontologists dubbed a *Primigenius Eliphas*. In fact, the creature now facing us shared some similarities with an elephant, except that it was squatter, and its legs knotty and bent, ending up with razor-sharp claws, instead of being straight, massive and stubby.

It also had a tail that ended with a diamond-shaped sting, but instead of moving back and forth like that of an Earth feline, it writhed as if it was a snake endowed with its own will. And perhaps it was...

Try to picture in your mind an apocalyptic hybrid of an elephant and a lion, and you might just have an idea of the abominable monster that was stalking us, and the sight of which had turned my blood to ice.

His jade-colored eyes had the disturbing stare of the mighty boa constructor when it is trying to hypnotize its prey.

After letting out one more bellowing roar, even louder than the one before, the monster eyed us for an uncomfortably long time. I could hear it sniffing, undoubtedly trying to identify our unknown smells, while its deadly tail kept rising furiously in the air. Then, it must have made up its mind, for it suddenly crouched down, like tigers do when they prepare to jump.

I was under no illusion that we could survive the encounter.

Of course, we could have tried running away towards the safety of the *Cosmos*, but it was perfectly obvious that the beast would catch up with us before we took ten steps.

Doctor Omega, as always, appeared inhumanly calm. His courage and composure before danger was for me a constant source of amazement. He clutched his spyglass as if it were a weapon, almost as if he could kill the monster with it.

Then it dawned on me that he was not clutching it aimlessly, but was using it to confuse the animal!

By reflecting the pale light of the sun and bouncing it back, like a child playing with a mirror, the Doctor had created a tiny patch of light that he used to distract the creature; he kept moving it gently before the monster's eyes, thereby diverting its attention.

The beast followed the sun spot and, once or twice, tried to grab it with its claws with lightning fast movements, but to no avail of course.

That clever trick kept the creature occupied, and bought us more time, but we dared not move lest the monster's attention focus on us again.

"M'sieur Borel," Fred said suddenly, "give me your cane!"

Without asking why, I handed the big man the metal bar that I had taken to use as my alpenstock.

Then, the brave lad stepped forward and, without any hesitation, slowly advanced towards the creature, while grabbing the rod firmly in his hand.

I confess that I was awed by his bravery. Even though a part of me considered his temerity to be pure folly, I could not help admiring his courage. Until now, I had thought of Fred as a last-minute addition to our crew, a negligible quantity, a laborer to whom menial and undemanding tasks could be delegated at no great cost. I was now forced to revise my opinion, and saw him under quite a different light.

At this fateful moment, Fred had become a hero. He had dared single-handedly confront a terrifying creature that could surely crush him with a single blow.

Yet, he kept moving forward, stepping cautiously, ready to strike with the metal bar should the monster lunge at him.

I feared the worst when I thought I saw the beast coil itself back, as if preparing to leap forward. I closed my eyes to avoid seeing what I was sure would be a ghastly spectacle. In my head, I already saw the beast's mighty claws rend my companion's body... I imagined him lifeless, torn and gutted, lying in a pool of blood while the savage mastodon was feasting upon his flesh...

110

Instead, what I first heard was a sharp sound, like that of a cane hitting a pillow. It was immediately followed by an admirative gasp from the Doctor.

I opened my eyes and was stupefied by what I beheld.

Fred had used my cane indeed, but only to slap his large hand with it, creating the noise that I had heard. I now recalled that I had seen lion-tamers use the same trick to dominate and impose their wills upon their animals. And it seemed to be working on Mars as well as it ever did on Earth.

I managed to suppress a victorious yell when I saw that the monster was now slowly backing away before Fred, keeping its head low, and emitting only a soft, wary growl. Each time the beast showed any sign of wanting to move forward again, or when its rumbling grew more threatening, Fred loudly slapped his hand, and took another cautious step forward.

The monster kept yielding ground, until finally, it surrendered totally to Fred's will; he turned tail and ran away into the hills.

Our friend let out a deep sigh of relief, and wiped the sweat off his brow. The Doctor and I rushed to congratulate him.

"I had no idea you had such skills, Fred," the scientist said.

"Well, I did spend a summer apprenticing at the *Cirque Medrano* in Paris," the big man replied. "I was hired only to lug bales of hay for the elephants and quarters of meat for the lions, but I still picked up a clue or two from the trainers. It's lucky I remembered some of their tricks."

"And very fortunate that it worked on such an alien monster," I added.

"If the dwarves we met earlier are his usual prey," the Doctor observed, "it must have grown unused to encountering any serious resistance."

"I bet you're right, Doctor," Fred said. "Those creepy little things must be like oysters to that big ugly creature..."

"And I wager it's not too often that it must have encountered someone as impressive as you, Fred," I added, smiling.

The big man almost blushed, and shrugged off the compliment.

Meanwhile, the Doctor was quickly jotting down a few notes in his diary.

"Did you see how fast that creature moved, Borel?" he asked. "Make a note of it. On Earth, an animal of that size would be slow and lumbering, like a rhinoceros perhaps. But here on Mars, it is much faster, because of the lower gravity. I'm starting to think that Martian fauna grows much faster than what we're used to, and is much more savage too... We'll have to be quite cautious during the rest of our journey."

We then decided to proceed towards the red hill that was our intended destination. But as we reached it, Fred drew our attention to another stupefying sight.

"Look over there!"

We looked in the direction he indicated, and discovered a valley of wonderful, prodigious beauty, hidden between two foothills.

Before us stood an azure plain, bordered by an avalanche of rocks that seemed to include all the colors of the rainbow!

Any one of our great impressionists would have been thrilled by the sight of those purple fields, framed by blue, yellow and green boulders. But we were not famous artists, only mere travellers, and could only gawk at such natural beauty.

I even wondered if I was not suffering from some kind of daltonism or another form of color blindness that might be distorting my sight, but a quick check indicated that both the Doctor and Fred saw the same thing as I.

As we took a few cautious steps towards what I had come to think of as the Enchanted Valley, we began to hear creaking sounds.

"What's that?" I asked the Doctor.

"Trees growing," he replied.

I laughed, but the scientist just stared at me.

"Why are you laughing?" he said.

"Because of what you just said... To hear trees growing... It's funny."

"But it is the truth, young man... Look!"

Indeed, as I stared at the ground, I saw a strange growth digging its way through the rocky ice, something that looked like purplish pods that burst with a snap under the rays of the sun, revealing the embryo of a tree, which in turn grew at an amazing pace.

The stem became a stalk, then a thin, weed-like trunk on which mauve, pearl-like buds shone gently, before opening slowly to sprout little silver branches, which gradually transformed into small bushels of triangular leaves.

When fully-grown, the trunk of these plants looked not unlike our cacti, thick, swollen, almost fleshy in appearance. These bushes grew very quickly all around us.

"Take note of all this, Borel," urged the Doctor. "The Martian flora is just as interesting as its fauna. I believe that these plants are like the mayflies of Earth; they're born in the morning and rise under the action of sunlight, then wither at night, releasing seeds that will give rise to another generation the next day, and so on... Extraordinary!"

I felt I could have been dreaming, and pinched myself to make sure I was not. An opium smoker could not have beheld in his fevered trance a more dazzling array of new visions as I had during our journey.

Having entered the valley, we marveled at the sight of its multi-colored vegetation, its shrubberies of scarlet, pink, purple and yellow fruits and flowers. The bushes had now grown into trees as tall as eucalyptus trees on Earth. A mere couple of hours ago, we had landed on a cold and desolate icy beach; now we stood in the midst of a splendid, multi-colored forest.

Everything I saw unarguably contradicted the statements I had read by the German philosopher Kant who, in the 18th century, had claimed that Mars was likely to carry the same forms of life as Earth.

The Doctor confided that one thing still puzzled him: except for the dwarves and the monster we had encountered earlier, we had met no other living beings on the surface. No birds, no small rodents, not even insects.

As we progressed through the forest, however, we began to hear faint, distant rumblings, like the muffled yawns or groans of something that lived deep within these woods. We eyed each other warily.

The Doctor's scientific curiosity was strong; he wanted to push further, travel deeper into the jungle to discover the origin of these noises. But neither Fred nor I were inclined to tempt fate.

"I came here to explore, not to turn tail at the first sign of danger," said the scientist petulantly.

"Yes, but you also said that we should be cautious," I reminded him. "We're not armed. Whatever this may be, we're not equipped to face it."

"M'sieur Borel is right, Doctor," said Fred. "If the thing that keeps making that noise ate all of the birds and little creatures that live around here, I don't think I can chase him away with my stick."

The Doctor harrumphed a little, but had no choice but to see the reason in our arguments.

So we turned back and retraced our steps towards the *Cosmos*.

But as we walked back through the forest, we began to suddenly feel very tired. Our limbs felt strangely heavy. We could barely keep our eyes open, and were fighting an invincible torpor that threatened to engulf us.

The Doctor was the first to stumble, falling to his knees, unable to get up.

Even though I was growing desperately short of breath myself, I rushed to his help, but as I did so, I felt as if life itself was being drained away from my body. While trying to get him up, we both fell heavily on the ground, like two drunken men.

Fred, whose constitution was far more robust than ours, was less affected than we were, even though his own efforts to remain standing would have seemed comical, if our situation had not been so tragic.

"What's happening to us, Doctor?" I asked in a daze. But the old scientist was barely conscious enough, and could not reply.

Fred grabbed each of us by the back of our coats, and dragged us like two sacks of potatoes, one heavy step at a time, until we were out of that accursed valley.

The feeling of torpor then dissipated, as unexplainably as it had come, and we were soon back on our own two feet.

"It must be the trees," said the Doctor, finally answering my question. "They exude a subtle vapor, or a pollen perhaps, that almost killed us... Like the Mance-nillier of the West Indies, a nice shade tree whose sheer toxicity can kill a man if he unwarily falls asleep under it. That Martian vegetation obviously shares some of the same characteristics. Had we stayed a minute longer in that forest, we could have become fodder for the things that live in it..."

I shuddered at the thought, but the effects of the mysterious poison vanished quickly and we briskly continued our trek back to the ship.

An icy wind had now risen, blowing at ground level, chilling us to the bone, making the journey uncomfortable, if not almost painful.

As we approached our craft, which was where we had left it on the icy beach, we experienced another shock. We saw that it was surrounded by a horde of dwarves that seemed to be desperately trying to find their way in.

"By all the Saints in Heaven!" cursed Fred. "The little rats are trying to break into the ship!"

Without thinking twice, Fred rushed at the creatures, his stick raised high. Either these were Martians who had not encountered us before, or they were braver than I suspected, for instead of running away, as I would have expected them to do, they actually held their ground.

Two of them even jumped at Fred, who swatted them back.

"Don't kill them if you can avoid it," urged the Doctor.

"I'll do my best, Doctor, but they don't let go easily," said Fred.

Heeding the Doctor's advice, our companion endeavored to grab the attacking Martians by their heads, as he would have snatched a bowling pin, and merely threw them back at the others.

"Listen to them, Borel," said the old scientist, a finger in the air. "They seem to speak in musical notes..."

To me, the high-pitched sounds uttered by the little creatures sounded like the cacophony produced by a mad orchestra, but once I began paying attention, I recognized the recurrence of four notes: *la*, *la*, *do* and *mi*!

While Fred was keeping the Martians at bay, the Doctor began to whistle the same notes, displaying a perfect pitch that I, an amateur musician, immediately envied. After a few tries, he must have hit the right combination, for I noticed that the dwarves suddenly stopped their crazed attacks.

Fred immediately dropped the creature he was holding in his massive hands; once released, the little being scurried back to his people.

I observed an even stranger phenomenon: the Martians began to change color, like chameleons. Their skin went from its previous pallid olive to a more saffron-like color, but I could not detect whether this change was a form of communication, or a reaction to an alien emotion like a blush on Earth.

The Doctor kept whistling the same basic notes, and the Martians disbanded peacefully, either running away or with little jumps like kangaroos. Soon they were all gone.

"Congratulations, Doctor. What did you say to them?" I asked.

"I'm not sure. I think I managed to communicate the notion that we too were people, and that we meant them no harm, and this time I seem to have succeeded..."

"You're amazing."

Fred came back from having taken a closer look at our ship.

"And a good thing that you got them away when you did too, Doctor," he said. "A pack of wild rats couldn't have done more damage."

We stepped forward to examine the outer shell of the *Cosmos*. Fred was right. Amazingly as it seemed, the hull exhibited signs of deep scratches, gouges, and even chewing as if it had been gnawed by an acid-spewing creature.

At the thought that these dwarves could have irreparably damaged our craft, I blanched. Without the *Cosmos*, we could never return home. I would have been stranded on Mars forever. It would have meant a perpetual exile in these hostile lands, and very likely a not-too-distant demise.

For the first time, I became fully conscious that the journey of exploration that I had so lightly undertaken could turn out to be the last thing I embarked upon in my life.

What madness could have possessed me to leave the native Earth upon which I lived so comfortably to visit this desolate world where death lurked at every corner!

I sighed as I reminisced about my lovely Normandy cottage and my beautiful Stradivarius.

Meanwhile, the Doctor looked nervous again.

"I think we've seen enough of this area. I'm ready to go."

The Martian night was approaching and the wind had redoubled in intensity. The temperature was dropping by the minute. Even with our padded clothing, it was becoming insufferably cold.

We hurried back inside the ship. A few minutes later, its power diffused a soft warmth that reinvigorated our nearly frozen limbs. Fred used a small gasoline fire to prepare a hot meal, and we gratefully ingested the food.

Outside the portholes, a soft snow was now falling, looking like a fine white mist, covering the bleak landscape with an icy shroud.

"Do not fear," said the Doctor, eyeing me and guessing my thoughts. "It won't hamper our journey."

"Should we travel by night?" I asked.

"Why not? I would rather not stay a moment longer in these parts, not with all the dangers we've already encountered. Besides, if we leave tonight, we'll be able to cross the valley without having to force our way through its deadly vegetation, since it rises only during the day."

I could appreciate the justness of the Doctor's argument.

Following the scientist's instructions, Fred activated a lever. There was a loud clang, the hum of the engines, and the wheeled tracks began moving again.

Soon, we were speeding away towards new, unknown destinations.

Chapter Six
The Beasts of Mars

"Are we always going to be travelling at night?" complained Fred. "I was hoping to take some photographs."

Doctor Omega smiled.

The scientist was driving our vehicle at a speed that was greatly increased by the uncanny properties of our hull and the lighter Martian gravity.

"Show a little patience, Fred," he said. "You'll soon be able to indulge your fancy after we've left these northern lands. I'm confident that the lands further to the south will be more hospitable."

"Do you really think so, Doctor?" I asked.

"Undoubtedly, young man. The polar regions we just visited were wild, inhabited by aggressive lifeforms who could only survive in their inhospitable surrounding by displaying an unusual degree of hostility. This should change as we journey towards the equator."

The Doctor had switched on the powerful head-lights located at the front of the *Cosmos*, but we could barely identify the shapes we saw as we drove by.

We moved in what looked like a barren, grey-blue plain, devoid of life, barely lit by the Martian moons in the sky above.

I observed that Phobos shone down with a light about as intense as a quarter-Moon of Earth—not bright enough to illuminate, but sufficient to cast shadows. The smaller and more distant Deimos, on the other hand, was more like a very bright star than a moon.

We drove on for four hours without any incident to relieve the monotony of the journey, a fact for which I was grateful.

Fred and I took turns with the driving, between catching short naps in our quarters. The Doctor seemed as rested as ever, and again I marveled at the prowess of that amazing man.

We were discussing for the umpteenth time what sort of things we were likely to encounter in the south when suddenly I screamed.

The *Cosmos* was falling downhill at an alarming speed!

Despite the Doctor's efforts to brake and slow the course of our vehicle, the ship's acceleration was only increasing. It looked to me like we were going to crash at the bottom of some god-forsaken precipice.

I could no longer contain my frustration and shouted at the scientist.

"Damn it, Doctor! Weren't you looking ahead? Didn't it occur to you that we might fall off the edge of a cliff? If we crash, it's going to be your fault!"

I had barely finished uttering these angry words than the *Cosmos*, having reached level ground after barreling down the side of the mountain, returned to its normal course and speed.

The danger had passed.

"Young man," said the Doctor mockingly, "I don't think I've ever had a more timorous companion than you in all my travels. You'd get scared of your own shadow."

In spite of his air of superiority, I noticed that he, too, looked a bit pale. I guessed that he may have been shaken as much as I was, but did not show it.

"Come on, Doctor! I'm sorry for shouting at you, but admit it: you were just as scared as I was."

The old scientist sniffed somewhat contemptuously, but said nothing.

Nevertheless, I noticed that after that incident, his vigilance redoubled. His eyes never left the road, and he was attentive to every detail. He carefully monitored the horizon, even occasionally stopping and asking Fred and me to look at an object ahead to determine whether it was an obstacle that we should go around, or a stretch of terrain over which we should decrease our speed.

After another five hours, we had covered quite a long distance. The terrain had changed. The ground under our tracks was no longer of the ashy, muddy variety that we had seen on the foothills; it was now flat and solid. For the first time since we had left the northern regions, we occasionally saw small animals in the distance, but they fled when they saw our vehicle.

Because of the darkness, we could not tell exactly what they looked like. However, a few came close enough to our headlights for us to take a good look at them. What we saw looked strange beyond belief. They looked like small, winged kangaroos.

Finally, dawn came.

We were now driving on a vast, red plain, steeped with a slow incline.

As we continued, the landscape began to change again. Everywhere, we saw strange-looking bushes rising from between the patches of snow that were already melting under the rays of the sun. Here and there, a few cacti had survived the freezing cold of the Martian night.

As it rose, the sun added new hues of yellow and blue to this monotonous plain.

The Doctor pointed at a jagged line that we could barely see on the horizon. It was hard to tell what it was. It could have been a forest, or a plantation of some kind.

"Don't you think we should take a closer look at this? It looks quite interesting, and different from the rest of this landscape."

"As you wish, Doctor."

I did not feel like raising an objection because I had understood that, when the Doctor was asking for someone else's opinion, it was merely his way of thinking aloud, and he never really listened to either advice or criticism.

That devil of a man was extremely inflexible in everything.

The *Cosmos* was now driving along smoothly, occasionally going over small, snow-filled ravines and mushy masses that crumbled softly under the weight of our vehicle. We seldom felt the bump of any obstacles.

In any event, the Doctor was so intent on reaching his goal that he would not have noticed it.

As we approached our destination, we could see that it was a sort of savanna or vast field of grass, covered with a grey-blue vegetation that looked like tall, pointy gladiola, sharp as knives.

Cautiously, Doctor Omega stopped the engines.

"This looks like a good place to stop and look around," he said.

Fred opened one of the side portholes, and let in some air from the outside. It felt warm and muggy, neither unpleasant nor uncomfortable.

We were about to step outside and leave the craft when Fred suddenly pointed at a silvery line that he saw zigzagging through the tall grass.

"Doctor! Look over there. It looks like... the grass is moving."

Indeed, it did look like the grass was being agitated by infrequent undulations and I thought I saw some mysterious sparkles move in and out of the vegetation.

The Doctor, frowning, studied the phenomenon for a while, looking through his spyglass. Then, raising his eyebrows in surprise, he declared:

"They're snakes! Big snakes... It's their scales that we see shining in the sun..."

He had barely finished his words than one of those hideous things attempted to slither up the sides of the *Cosmos* and we had to hurriedly close the porthole.

They were indeed reptiles of some kind, but in truth, I had never seen such gigantic, horrible snakes before.

They had pointy, triangular heads. Their bodies were deep purple with large black, brown or steel blue spots on the back, and pinkish bellies. Their middle sections were crossed by white bands separated by red and green rings.

They were at least sixty feet in length. Their protractile tongues were attached to their palates by a twin cartilage, and the forks kept jutting in and out of their mouths. Their lidless eyes were a deep crimson red. At the other end of their sinewy, tubular bodies was a tail not unlike that of a fish.

While gnashing and thrashing against our ship, those monsters made a sibilant hiss that pierced our ears.

It looked like the sight of the *Cosmos* had first frightened them, but then seeing that our craft remained motionless, they grew bolder and were slithering all over us.

We were surrounded by a living sea of snakes that curled around us, and even managed to jump into the air to better stare at us with their blood-colored eyes.

The Doctor was beginning to look concerned. As for me, I do not mind admitting that I was terrified; I had even begun to shake uncontrollably.

"Could they break into the ship?" I asked the scientist.

"Probably not, but truthfully, I don't know what these animals are capable of. We should leave, but there are so many of them I'm afraid they'd gum up the wheels... And then where would we be, hmm?"

I was scared beyond words. I could never have imagined the horror of our current predicament. I confess that, at that moment, I almost wished we had been smashed by the helix, or killed by the underwater warriors of the Sea of Ice.

I had always felt a terrible repugnance towards snakes... I remembered that, when I was but a boy, I fainted at the sight of an ordinary grass snake. My readers can easily picture the state of panic which I felt.

The Martian snakes were slithering all over the *Cosmos*, crawling on our hull, our wheels, and their numbers kept growing by the minute.

I curled up in a fetal position on my seat and tried not to look at the horrible things that obscured our portholes; I was bathed in a cold sweat.

But I was suddenly awakened from my torpor by the Doctor's clipped, unhurried, authoritative voice.

"Fred! Go to the store room and fetch some flares!"

I then recalled that, among the supplies we had taken with us, were rockets in the event that we had to signal our position to some would-be rescuers. I did not think at the time that we would need them, but I was wrong, since they turned out to be very useful, although not for their original purpose.

Once the big man had returned with his cargo, the Doctor carefully lit one flare, then acting with a speed that belied his age, quickly opened a porthole, threw it out, and slammed it shut.

Almost immediately, there was a shower of sparks, an initial loud explosion, followed by several smaller ones.

The Martian snakes began to flee in panic, slithering back to their sea of grass as far as they could. To be on the safe side, the Doctor and Fred each released one more flare on either side of the *Cosmos*. The ophidian horde that had paralyzed us was now in full rout. The undulations of the grass showed that the snakes could not wait to put a wide distance between themselves and us.

"Let's take advantage of this and get out of here fast," said the Doctor.

The path ahead was now free of obstacles, snakes or otherwise, and the *Cosmos* quickly gained speed.

Minutes later, we had left the deadly savanna behind us, and we were driving alongside a flat landscape strewn with rocks made of a powdery, red chalk-like substance, broken only by steep, jagged crevices.

We often had to make considerable detours in order to avoid falling into one of these chasms.

The vegetation, which had been so luxuriant before, had now become sparse to the point of being desertic. I had seen photographs of North Africa that looked a little like what I saw outside our windows. There were very few trees, and only the occasional patch of the sharp, gladiola-like tall grass.

Eventually, the path became clearer and we could again accelerate.

Our journey southward continued, and the rest of the day passed without any further incident, much to my pleasure.

As night fell, we decided to pause and enjoy a much needed rest.

"Let's stop here," said the Doctor, choosing an area that was protected from the wind by several huge boulders and therefore offered a comfortable shelter.

Even though we were now much closer to the equator, the cold was still very intense outside. We enjoyed the warmth and comfort of our ship. Fred prepared us another excellent meal on his portable stove.

"During the night, I suggest we take watch in turn," said the Doctor. "We know nothing of the land outside and we shouldn't take any risks. One of us needs to stay awake at all times in order to warn the others, should an unexpected danger arise."

We ate with hearty appetite, and after a cup of tea laced with some good Jamaican rum, we set up our respective watch periods. The luck of the draw made me the first to be in charge of watching over the *Cosmos*.

Doctor Omega and Fred retired to their quarters, and soon I could hear the big man's loud snoring coming from his bunk.

I sat in the driver's seat, looking through the porthole into the darkness outside. As I could not see anything, I decided to turn down the lights in the cabin and sit in the dark, so that I could at least enjoy the sight of the Martian moons.

After what seemed to be an hour or so, I began to see small points of lights in the dark, flittering stars that appeared and disappeared, vanished then returned, sometimes burning with more intensity than before.

At first, I thought that my eyes were playing tricks on me, and I rubbed them vigorously. But the phenomenon did not stop—on the contrary.

The small reddish stars were hovering at ground level. I was intrigued by the phenomenon and wondered about its cause—could these be Martian will o' wisps?

A vague feeling of apprehension began to take hold of me.

I did not dare to wake my companions, yet I felt that a new danger could be threatening us. I had learned that one could expect anything on that uncharted planet.

I decided to get up and look through one of the side portholes. But there, I saw only the same small red stars floating in the dark.

Sometimes they glided barely a foot above the ground; at others, they shot up in the air in a zig-zag-like pattern, before descending, then rising again.

These were not will o' wisps, I thought. I was now sure of this. They were caused by something new and different. But what could that be?

Suddenly, I found the answer! I remembered my nightmare before our departure, and the cat which had been sleeping at the foot of my bed.

The red stars were the eyes of Martian wildcats!

I peered more closely through the darkness, and now I thought I could make out the contours of some fantastic beasts skulking through the shadows. My over-active imagination even enabled me to hear their hungry breathing, although I knew that was entirely in my mind.

As the eyes grew and multiplied around the *Cosmos*, I could no longer stand it and decided to wake my companions.

"What is it this time, Borel?" said Doctor Omega tetchily.

He was about to turn on the lights in the cabin when I stopped him and whispered:

"Look outside."

He stuck his face to the window and peered into the dark, as impassible as a stone statue.

"Curious," he said after a long while.

Then, after another pause, he continued:

"Undoubtedly, young man, you've awakened me to look at these... wild beasts... These dots of lights are their eyes... I think I can even see the shape of their bodies creeping around on the ground..."

As he said this, a chorus of howls began. Somehow, the animals had either sensed our movements, or perhaps heard our voices... They made a terrifying din, worse than a pack of Siberian wolves.

"Let's see if we can scare them away too," said the Doctor with his characteristic composure.

130

"Are you going to use more flares?"

"I don't think it'll be necessary."

The Doctor switched on the bright lights at the front of the *Cosmos*.

A flood of light swamped our neighborhood.

We then could see the beasts that had been surrounding us: they were like black panthers with flat heads and shiny teeth. They panicked and jumped away like frogs in a mad rush, growling and yelping, hissing like steam boilers gone amuck. In less than a minute, they had all vanished back to where they came from.

The plain was silent once more, devoid of any signs of life.

I was of the opinion that we should leave immediately, but the Doctor disagreed.

"Would you prefer to face yet another new peril, Borel?" he admonished me. "You saw how easily we scared away these cats, hmm? They won't come back now, and even if they do, we can throw a few flares at them. No, we're better off spending the rest of the night here."

Then, he patted me kindly on the shoulder and said in a more friendly tone:

"Go and get some rest, young man. I'll take the next watch."

I did not argue with him this time, and gladly retired to my quarters.

In less time than it took me to write this sentence, I fell asleep. I sank into a deep, restorative slumber, escaping at last from all the emotions that I had experienced during the day.

When I woke up, it was already mid-day, and the *Cosmos* was driving at high speed on an immense prairie, flat as a billiard table.

The vegetation had changed again. The hostile flora from before had been replaced by a vast expanse of pink grass with scatterings of yellow, green and blue flowers. I even saw little streams that filled swamp-like ponds, bordered by weird-looking trees, whose trunks were like polished marble and almost without branches.

A hushed whisper seemed to imbue that world... A deep and melancholic sound that evoked a faint moan or a series of whimpers... After a while, we became convinced that it was merely an effect of the wind.

Around us low altitude clouds rolled in. We drove through their thick, white masses and, through that thin mist, we saw a range of mauve hills and valleys in the distance. These were sprinkled from place to place with daubs of purple and pink, green and orange...

I was soon spellbound by the enchanted scenery.

Even Fred, who was not particularly appreciative of matters of aesthetics, kept raving about the marvels we beheld. The same word kept returning to his lips.

"It's like a fairyland!"

And he was right—it was just like a fairyland.

There was nothing in all the cosmos, I thought, that could equal the shining splendor of this far-away place... The unsettling majesty of this unending solitude...

The *Cosmos* was speeding along this enchanting countryside, when suddenly the Doctor, who was again doing the driving, turned around and asked us to come closer.

"Young man... Fred... Take a look at that, on the horizon... Tell me what you see... It looks like a herd on the march, hmm? But are they people—or animals?"

I squinted to get a better look at the tiny dots the Doctor indicated.

"I don't think they're people," I said, after observing them for a while. "They would be too big. The people we've met before were all fairly small."

Fred, ever the pragmatic, used the Doctor's spyglass.

"I'll be damned," he said. "They're elephants–or things that look just like them!"

Doctor Omega steered the *Cosmos* in that direction, and soon we could satisfy our curiosity. Less than three hundred feet away, we discovered what indeed looked like a herd of pachyderms on the move.

As we got closer, the huge beasts stopped and began to stare at us.

The Doctor turned the wheel and the *Cosmos* made a prudent turn, maintaining a safe distance between us and those Martian giants.

They looked more like prehistoric mastodons than modern elephants; their fur was a deep purple, and their tails, ears and trunks were black. They sported two pairs of curved tusks on either side of their mouth, and their front legs were bizarrely longer than their hind legs.

They must have mistaken our ship for another animal, for suddenly they rushed at us, snorting like seals emerging from water.

"They don't look that fierce," remarked Fred.

"You're probably right, but we don't want them to collide with us," replied the Doctor. "If they damaged the *Cosmos*, how would we repair it, hmm?"

We sped away and soon, the pachyderms became only a small purple line on the horizon, and eventually vanished from our sight entirely.

As we kept driving south, the temperature increased. It was now twelve degrees Celsius and, after the

Siberian cold of the northern regions, we enjoyed this more temperate weather to the fullest.

Far to our right, I saw the silhouette of a mountain range. The prairie had changed once more: the grass was now far more red than pink, and the scattered vegetation looked distinctly different, although the marble trees (as I called them) still littered the landscape like a graveyard of Grecian columns.

I heard the characteristic sound of rushing water, and soon we came across a frothy torrent that had come crashing down from the mountains to end in a great lake. Strange beasts swam on its mirror-like surface. From a distance, they looked like swans, but as we got closer we discovered that they were nothing like these beautiful animals.

Try imagining birds with small heads shaped like sharks', sharp, jagged wings and long, flexible necks, and you will have an image of what these peculiar creatures looked like.

"Yuck... What ugly things," said Fred, indicating his distaste with a grimace. "And look over there! What are those ugly birds crawling all over that tree?"

Our companion had directed our attention towards a grove of marble trees near the lake, located straight ahead of us. It appeared inhabited by a flock of strange, flying creatures.

"Are you certain they're birds?" said the Doctor. "Look at their hands and feet."

"That's right," I said, as we got closer. "They look like they have human heads."

"I think they're man-bats," said the scientist. "Huge man-bats."

"Like vampires?" said Fred, taking a step back, suddenly looking frightened.

"Perhaps. I want to take a closer look at them," replied the Doctor, oblivious to any concerns for our safety.

He drove the *Cosmos* to the boundaries of the strange grove, then stopped the vehicle to study the frightening creatures. We were now close enough that we could examine them in great detail.

Their bodies were squat and ovoid in shape; their skin was reddish, covered with patches of white fur. Their thoraxes were large and inflated, and supported two powerful arms. Under them, they wore a light purple membrane that, once unfolded, made for a pair of long, chitinous, triangular wings.

Their heads were as hideous and terrifying as I could ever have imagined. They were round and shiny, like old ivory. Their faces were a pallid green, with two round red eyes covered by a nictitating membrane that opened and shut rapidly. They had no nose to speak of, only two slits, and their mouths were like blood-red gashes across their faces.

Their pointy tongue darted incessantly in and out of their mouths, and I could even see small, but sharp and pointed teeth.

Even though I felt safe inside the *Cosmos*, I could not look at these creatures without feeling a reawakening of all of Mankind's ancient terrors.

They looked like the ancient devils that had terrified our species since its prehistory. They were so repulsive and savage-looking that, even today, I still have nightmares about them.

Suddenly, two of these vampires took flight and came to land on top of our vehicle. I shuddered as I heard the sound of their clawed feet scratch and crawl above our heads.

Doctor Omega paid them no attention but continued to study them with his spyglass. He pointed at the grove.

"Borel! Fred! Look over there! It looks like huts! What a fascinating sight!"

Indeed, I noticed several ocher-colored hives, tied together by a mesh of vines, a few feet above the ground on the trunks of the trees... It was the man-bats' homes... They looked like dome-covered baskets, with their sides coated with a yellow gummy substance. The orifice that served as their entrance was oval-shaped and surprisingly decorated with beautiful, primitive carvings.

The Martian vampires had suddenly been revealed, much to my surprise, to be intelligent beings, gifted with artistic sensibilities.

"The dwarves we met earlier were nothing more than savages," said the Doctor, paralleling my thoughts. "These beings, on the other hand, appear to be far more civilized and capable of artistic expression... How remarkable!"

"But will they be friendly?"

"We shall have to see."

"They're so... scary."

"Life in the universe can take many shapes, young man," said the Doctor. "There are creatures in the universe who may look like demons to you, and yet they are wise and benevolent. Take these people for instance... There's one thing about them you haven't noticed, hmm?"

"What?"

"Those membranes that made us initially believe they were bat-like beings are entirely man-made."

"Really?"

"Look at that hive over there," said the Doctor, handing me his spyglass.

I then realized that he was quite correct. I saw two Martians use their skeletal hands to adjust the winged membranes under their arms. Those repulsive, terrifying beings had discovered the secret of flight, and found a way to soar through the air like birds!

As I kept studying what I now called the Hanging Village, I saw other creatures, more delicate ones– probably their females–busy manufacturing new membranes out of a flat vine that looked like an algae. They cut long triangular patches which they assembled into new wings for their male companions.

"Look at that. They're making wings. They're so smart!" I exclaimed.

"I can't say I'm surprised," said Fred, sounding inordinately pleased with himself. "I figured that one already."

"And how did you do that?"

"Look at the way they look at us. The dwarves we met north weren't much better than animals. But these vampires have a crafty look in their eyes. They remind me of a pig farmer who lives in Le Neubourg, and always cheats his customers. I wouldn't trust them farther than I could throw them. Look! They even smoke like regular folks."

Fred was right. I could see that two of the man-bats sitting outside their huts were puffing with an obvious air of pleasure on something that looked like an elongated pipe.

"I'd be mighty interested in trying some of their tobacco," mused Fred.

In the meantime, other man-bats had taken flight and landed on top of the *Cosmos*, gesticulating and making noises that reminded me of peacock screams.

The Doctor was debating whether we should go, or stay and try to communicate with these beings, when it occurred to me that they were actually trying not to attack us, but to warn us about something.

I followed the direction of their eyes and glanced at the ground, which was more visible from one of the side portholes.

I let out a scream of horror at what I saw!

The ground was almost entirely carpeted with thick, black snakes that writhed and twisted in awful convulsions. There were hundreds—what am I saying?—thousands of them...

"Let's get out of here, Doctor! Fast!"

For once, the scientist agreed with me. The *Cosmos* moved forward, squishing the awful beasts. We had to go into fourth gear to get enough traction to reach a normal driving speed.

When we finally reached safer ground, the Doctor observed:

"Now we know why these beings developed wings. Their land is plagued by snakes, although from what I saw, I think these were more like worms. To avoid them, the natives have built their houses in those shiny trees that the worms can't climb. They also designed wings enabling them to travel and hunt. Very clever of them..."

It occurred to me that the more we travelled south, the more advanced were the inhabitants we encountered. Until then, we had easily triumphed over all the obstacles this uncharted world had thrown in our path. But what would the future bring? Would not more advanced Martians be capable of building something far more sophisticated than mere wings? Deadly, powerful engines of destruction perhaps?

It was obvious, after all that we had seen, that Mars was inhabited by many intelligent beings. I feared that all our resources might ultimately prove ineffective against the next race we would encounter...

Chapter Seven
The City of Fire

The *Cosmos* had finally reached civilization.

As we sped south along the Martian plains, I sensed that we were approaching an actual city.

The landscape that I saw through the portholes of our craft was no longer wild and untamed. Instead, I beheld what looked like cultivated fields, regular squares of vegetation of different colors, lined up according to patterns that remained a mystery. Yellow strips here, red rectangles there, purple, blue, orange or rust-colored squares a little further away...

I was sure that it was not one of Nature's caprices that had distributed these colors and made these geometric shapes. Only an intelligence could have organized them so.

However, I was surprised to not detect the presence of any living beings. I could see no farmers, no workers tilling in these fields.

Strangely, I occasionally saw the ground move, heaving up and down, as if it were being plowed from underneath by some prodigious tool.

Upon further scrutiny, I noticed that there were, in fact, some machines moving about inside the fields, slowly making progress along their lengths, separated by distances of about eighty feet from each other... They looked like flatbed, metal chariots, but I could see no Martians inside or on top of them. Yet, they must have been guided by some intelligence, for they moved according to intricate patterns... If they were plows of some kind, I could not understand what made them run.

"The people who designed these machines are obviously technologically advanced," said Doctor Omega. "I'd be inclined to think that they must be as weak as the people we've met before, but that they've created powerful robots to compensate... Machine power replacing physical strength... Very clever... Everything we see here appears to be completely automatic... I'm curious to meet these people and discover what else they're capable of..."

Needless to say, I did not quite share the Doctor's enthusiasm, but kept my counsel. While he spoke, I remained glued to the porthole and looked with a mixture of puzzlement and anxiety at the multi-colored horizon that lay ahead of us, wondering what fate had in store for us.

As we kept driving, the sun began to sink slowly beyond the mountain line.

Suddenly, I gasped in surprise.

Just ahead of us, the sky was crisscrossed by streaks of light, moving up and down like lanterns held in the hand of an invisible giant.

Sometimes, they burned as bright as a flash of lightning, other times, they were paler, yellowish green.

At first, I thought that we had reached a mountain on the sides of which Martian climbers carried torches... But when I took a second look, I realized that there were no mountains. The land before us was as flat as ever. Besides, I could see other, identical lights further ahead. So I kept studying that strange phenomenon, trying to fathom its origins.

"You're wondering what's the source of those lights, hmm?" said the Doctor.

"Well, yes, I am."

"Look again. They go up and down. In straight lines and circles."

"Yes, they do. I noticed that."

"Doesn't that suggest anything to you, young man?"

"Well, er..."

"Flight. Those lights are controlled by flying creatures!"

"You mean, like those bat-folks we met yesterday?" said Fred, jumping to his feet.

"No... I don't think so," replied the Doctor, carefully considering his answer. "They would be gliding in the sky, instead of performing real aerial maneuvers like these..."

We kept looking at the lights, and finally our patience was rewarded.

A streak of fire came sufficiently close to the *Cosmos* that we could clearly notice the shape of two giant flaming wings.

"They're... firebirds," said the Doctor in awe.

"What a sight," muttered Fred. "Light birds instead of lamp posts... How are we going to top that? *Sacrebleu*, Doctor, I'm glad you let me come with you and see all these marvels... I don't regret a minute of this trip..."

The mercurial big man had quickly forgotten some of the perils we had already faced...

But my attention was suddenly caught by another, even more bewildering spectacle. In the distance ahead, I began seeing streams of blue flames shooting up in the air at regular intervals, like the illuminated fountains at the Palace of Versailles.

I also heard a mysterious, low, rumbling noise, so loud that it even penetrated the hull of our craft. I recognized it: it was the sound of mighty machines pumping and striking in unison as part of some giant industrial enterprise.

"What do you thinks this means?" I asked the Doctor.

"Clearly, we're approaching a city–a vast industrial powerhouse, from what it seems..."

"Should we stop now?"

"And miss seeing it? Absolutely not!" replied the scientist indignantly.

We were about a mile away from the place that sprouted the giant blue flames, which like clockwork, kept illuminating the darkness outside.

The sound of the machines–or what I assumed were machines–had grown to become deafening. My God! What a racket! The Cyclops themselves could not have made more noise forging Zeus' thunderbolts.

Except for the blue flames, the night was total, yet the din continued.

"Obviously, the work goes on," remarked the Doctor. "It must be automated."

"No eight-hour day for them Martians! Ha!" said Fred, who obviously did not care much for our new labor laws.

To be on the safe side, we had slowed down, but suddenly a violent commotion shook our entire ship and sent us spinning through the cabin. We felt the ground quake, and I saw tongues of blue fire burst around us only a few feet away.

We had mistakenly driven right into the midst of one of these flaming jets. They looked like the will o' wisps that one sees in swamps or graveyards, but a hundred time larger and brighter. They were crowned by what looked like an egret made of light, or perhaps the top of a pomegranate...

Now the *Cosmos* was surrounded by violent bursts of fire that leaped into the air like a jack in the box, and writhed like snakes. It was like driving through a mine field. Maybe the Martians were collecting energy from the core of their planet in the same fashion as we humans drill for oil or natural gas?

Doctor Omega skillfully drove the *Cosmos* between those geysers of blue fire. Now more alert than ever, he displayed marvelous skills and managed to avoid them all; only once our twice was our ship brushed–and then, only barely–by the fiery jets.

But our situation was growing ever more desperate. Realistically, it was only a matter of time before the *Cosmos* was hit again. We had to leave that circle of fire before it destroyed us.

Further on in the darkness, I spotted a garland of bright red points of lights, and electric-blue disks that spun rapidly in the midst of a shower of sparks.

I figured that it was yet another enigmatic, mind-boggling factory built by this highly advanced people that we had yet to meet. It looked like an assemblage of powerful, complex, ominous machinery, the purpose of which I could not fathom.

It was probably pure folly to think of seeking refuge there, especially at night, but what other choice did we have?

The Doctor, as usual, harbored no doubts as to the right course of action. He was one of those men always all too happy to jump from the frying pan into the fire, and from the fire into an even more awful peril.

"Let's go forward!" he said, casting a last, quick glance behind us, and grabbing the wheel even more firmly.

I had the sinking feeling that going forward and entering that alien factory was to step into the jaws of death... But to continue on our present path was to eventually fall victim to the geysers of blue fire, the number and intensity of which seemed to only be increasing.

I was terrified by the colossal and dark machines that roared and clanged around us as we drove into the industrial complex. I thought we might be shredded by the strange spinning metal disks, or crushed by the weight of the metal pylons which, like hammers, fell upon their anvils with the strength of titans.

Once we entered the factory, even our own powerful headlights paled before the bright, burning light that surrounded us, a light like that of a blazing inferno. In spite of the night outside, I could clearly study all the details of its construction.

I saw what looked like great metal bridges and gigantic scaffoldings... Streams of a strange, boiling, milky-white liquid rushed past us in iron gutters, and emitted a mist that gave the landscape an eerie air of unreality, like some nightmarish vision of hell...

As we moved deeper into this city of fire, the sound of the jackhammers became even more deafening, as incredible as it may be to imagine. It was like the sound of millions of anvils being hammered at the same time. We were beginning to reel from the assault on our nerves.

The industrious activity of this bizarre metropolis that never slept went on constantly, while we desperately sought a way out, innocent mice trapped inside an inhuman metal maze.

Suddenly, somewhere in that mad entanglement of girders and beams, causeways and rafters, I noticed small gnome-like silhouettes scurrying around like rats. They were moving rapidly, almost defying gravity, performing incomprehensible tasks, occasionally gathering to confer in groups of twos and threes.

These were surely the master-builders of the fantastic city we had entered. I immediately pointed them out to my companions.

Doctor Omega stopped the *Cosmos*. We deliberated as to whether we should do something to attract their attention. The scientist was in favor of it, and so was Fred, so certain was the big man of the Doctor's wisdom and of his own strength. I was not so sanguine, but I knew that we were lost in that hellish factory, and would never get out without help. So I went along with the majority view, while secretly girding myself for the worst.

The Doctor used our front headlights to signal the creatures.

At first, nothing happened. I had begun to think that his signal had not been noticed, when suddenly, we were struck by a bolt of intense, bright light!

At the same time, we began feeling a sharp increase in the temperature inside the ship.

From what I could see through the porthole, the bolt came from a cumbersome machine that looked like a giant projector, and that had been moved into position behind us by an entire cadre of Martians.

It was now pointing straight at us, beaming its deadly luminescence at the *Cosmos*.

Do not ask me to explain how our ship, which had weathered the absolute cold of space, could now be affected by outside temperature. This was more than a mere heat ray. When I touched the hull, it was as cold as ever. It was the air inside the ship that was being heated! What kind of trickery these fiendish Martians used, I shall never know, although the Doctor mentioned microscopic waves or some kind–explanations I barely understood.

Soon, we began to experience difficulty breathing... Each intake of air burned the insides of my nose and my lungs.

The Doctor tried to start the engines again, but discovered that the road ahead of us had been blocked by a hastily arranged barricade of metal girders. Our right and our left were obstructed by canals of white, boiling liquid. And to turn back, assuming we could have maneuvered the *Cosmos* without encountering further obstacles, would have meant facing the wall of blue flames.

The Martians had us effectively trapped, each avenue of escape made impossible by the hostile environment of their monstrous city.

Inside the ship, the temperature now reached 62 degrees Celsius (over 140 F). The concentrated beam of light seemed to increase in intensity by the minute.

I became convinced that the Martians meant to kill us, to roast us alive inside our craft as a chicken in a pot.

While I surrendered to my gloomy thoughts, the Doctor was now trying to pull the wheels back inside, and turn the *Cosmos* back into a spacecraft. I remembered our departure from Earth, and knew that if he could activate the mysterious stellite that covered our hull, we could fly over that accursed city, and perhaps leave that hellish world as well.

But I could tell by the look of frustration on his face that this was not going to happen.

"What's wrong?" I asked.

"Their beam appears to be interacting with the anti-gravitic properties of the stellite. If we try to take off now, we risk an explosion..."

"The ship would explode?"

"Yes. And likely the entire northern hemisphere of the planet as well," replied the Doctor, all too casually for my taste.

My mind could not grasp the magnitude of the devastation he described. I shook my head in incredulity.

"What choice do we have then?" I asked.

"We must abandon the ship," said the Doctor.

"Go out there?" I gasped.

"We don't have a choice, Borel. We can't leave. And if we stay in here, we'll die."

"I fear we're doomed either way, Doctor. If we surrender to these monsters, they'll likely kill us after putting us through all kinds of ghastly alien torture."

"Never, by God!" shouted Fred. "I'm not going to be led like a lamb to the slaughter. We'll sell our skins dearly. I didn't quite figure everything you said, Doctor, but I understood that we've got to shut off that magic lantern of theirs if we want to escape. Well, I'm the man to do it! And with this, I fear no one!"

The big man grabbed his iron-tipped walking stick, and made way towards the exit.

"Wait!" said the Doctor.

He rushed to his quarters and rummaged in a box he kept under his cot. Soon, he returned holding in his hands a small bulbous item that looked like a gun, but surprisingly did not have a traditional barrel. It ended with a single metal rod, with no hole through which a projectile might be shot.

"What is that?" I asked.

"It's a prototype *staseur*, a weapon developed by my people. It emits a strong energy discharge that incapacitates one's opponent, or worse. It will help you out there."

Fred made a face, the meaning of which was obvious. He did not like the new weapon.

"I don't know, Doctor... I prefer to stick with what I know..."

Making up my mind on the spot, I reached for the *staseur*.

"I haven't behaved very bravely until now," I told my two companions. "In fact, to speak frankly, I haven't been much of an asset to this expedition at all. The least I can do now is help Fred secure our freedom. This weapon of yours, Doctor, cannot be more difficult to handle than my old Smith & Wesson..."

I took the gun in my hand and felt its odd weight against my palm. It gave me a sense of comfort. The

Doctor showed me that I had to press a stud with my thumb to fire it, instead of pulling a trigger.

While we were getting ready, the heat inside the ship had continued to go up by a few more degrees. It was now as hot as a steam bath–without the stream.

"I'll be fine a little while longer," said the Doctor, noticing my air of concern. "I'm perhaps a little more resistant than you..."

In a flash, we had unbolted the door and jumped outside the ship.

By the time I stepped out, Fred had already sent more than a dozen Martians reeling back with swings of his stick. He rapidly moved forward, keeping our attackers at bay with vast circular swings.

"Gotcha!... You, you stay away if you know what's good for you... You're trying to catch me from behind eh, but it won't work, my fine fella!... Get a little taste of my stick..." he monologued in his rumbling voice while mowing down the gnomes foolish enough to tackle him.

As for me, I moved cautiously behind him, taking advantage of his cover while using the Doctor's gun to protect his back. I shot down the Martians that tried to attack us from the rear. The little creatures just collapsed when hit by the invisible electric discharge of the *staseur*.

Together, Fred and I cut quite a swath among the Martians and made good progress towards the beam projector.

When we reached the machine, it had already been abandoned by the gnomes that had scurried away before us. Its blinding beam was still directed towards our ship.

We walked carefully behind it and I noticed a control panel of some kind. Despite my apprehensions, Fred immediately hit it several time with his stick, until it was completely destroyed.

The beam of light vanished almost immediately.

To complete our mission, Fred also tried to break the front of the projector by hitting the crystalline lens that covered it several times, but was unable to break it.

During all of this, the Martians had vanished.

I tugged at Fred's sleeve.

"Let's not waste any more time," I suggested. "The beam is no more and we've wrecked the controls. Let's return to the ship."

We felt quite victorious and walked back towards the *Cosmos* like Olympians.

Unfortunately, our pride preceded our fall, quite literally. For suddenly, we stumbled and fell forward to the ground.

We tried to get up, but discovered that a web of almost invisible but unbreakable wires tied our limbs. The more effort we made to disentangle ourselves, the more we became enmeshed in it.

It appeared that the Martians had somehow managed to deposit a nearly invisible net made of some devilishly hard substance on the ground, and we had walked right into their trap!

Soon, we were caught like flies in a spider web, our arms and our legs totally immobilized....

It all happened so fast that we barely had time to comprehend what had taken place...

When we finally lay still and powerless on the ground, the Martians came skulking out of the shadows where they had been hiding. I heard the sound of a drill and felt a vibration. By twisting to one side, I saw that they had planted metal poles on either side of us, and from these had sprang more wires that now covered us completely.

We were well and truly prisoners, with no possible escape!

I was hoping to use the Doctor's *staseur*, which I still gripped in my right hand, to exact some revenge on the first gnome that would dare come within shooting distance of me, but even that was denied to me.

I suddenly felt a painful burning sensation on my hand, and discovered that it was caused by a red beam which one of the Martians was projecting at me from a little box that reminded me of a Kodak brownie camera.

I screamed in pain and released my grip on the *staseur*. Immediately, two of the little monsters lassoed it with their devilish wire, and dragged the weapon towards them. The sense of loss that filled me became so powerful that I was overwhelmed with rage and I began screaming like a madman.

Frightened, for my voice must have seemed formidable to these creatures, the Martians first quickly stepped back, readying themselves for a new assault. Then, realizing they had nothing to fear, they returned.

I heard their feet shuffling on the ground as they came closer. It was a soft, muffled sound, like the blood-curdling slither of a snake... They made mewling sounds like doves... Sometimes, that sound moved up and down the scale, alternating between a low rattle and a high pitch, which was rather odd and frightening.

I had placed my last hopes in Doctor Omega's ability to save us, using one of those unexpected miracles of which he had the secret. But these hopes were dashed when I saw the old scientist being led towards us by several gnomes pointing their deadly boxes at him.

They gestured at him to sit down on the ground, which he did, and they quickly lassoed him and tied him to the metal posts using their unbreakable wire. From where I lay, I could see his slick, white hair shining in the reddish glow of the Martian factory.

Then, they left us to our own devices, no doubt confident in the solidity of their bonds.

"Doctor... Doctor... So you're a prisoner too..."

My new-found courage collapsed at that instant and I let out a string of curses... I am not ashamed to admit that I even cried, like am angry child being denied what he wants by his parents...

Eventually, my tears yielded to my anger and my frustration.

"See where your foolish plans have got us?" I hurled at the Doctor. "Yes, you're a genius, but didn't it occur to you to take some guns to defend ourselves against the threats we might encounter? Any explorer would know that! How could you be so stupid? Because of you, we're all going to die here! And we'll be lucky if they don't torture us for hours beforehand! Damn you, Doctor! Damn you and your insane pride!"

The old scientist let out a deep sigh.

"I'm really sorry, Mister Borel. I should not have asked you to come with me. You're absolutely right. It was a stupid and self-centered thing to do..."

This was said with such heartfelt contrition that I now regretted my harsh words. In fairness, I realized that my old companion had not twisted my arm to force me to go with him. I could have chosen to stay home. I, and only I, was at fault here.

I started to mutter some embarrassed apologies, when Fred butted in.

"Don't lose hope, yet, M'sieur Borel," said the big man. "I know the Doctor. I've seen him pull out of tighter spots, eh, Doctor?"

But the scientist said nothing.

We remained prisoners all night, unable to move, unable to sleep.

At daybreak, the Martians returned, in greater number than before, and far more agitated. It was like a mad stampede, making a prodigious racket.

I guessed that the crowd had learned the news of our coming, and was now eager to see us... From time to time, I heard the noise of an engine, the sounds of wheels, of metal against metal... All that against the din of the factory... But I could see nothing...

Suddenly, I felt the wires that were tying me becoming loose... They no longer held me flat against the ground... The mesh that had been thrown over our bodies was removed... Only my arms and my legs were still tightly bound together...

With prodigious contortions, Fred and I managed to sit up, next to the Doctor.

Then I beheld an astounding scene that will forever remain etched in my memory.

The number of Martians gathered before us was like an ocean of bodies, stretching as far as the eye could see... A sea of faces... Thousands of these strange alien beings who were both like and yet unlike the other creatures we had met so far.

With the benefit of daylight, I could see that, even though these Martians looked equally small and fragile, they had obviously evolved beyond the savage state of their Nordic brethren, and also beyond that of the half-civilized tree-dwellers we had encountered earlier.

They, too, were about two feet high, with stick-like limbs and bulbous, moon-like heads. Their pallid, green skin seemed almost transparent, except for some darker green splotches around the slots that were their nostrils and their mouths.

But unlike the other creatures we had met, their round, lidless red eyes shone with the unmistakable signs of a high intelligence. I thought I could even detect a note of cold and cruel irony in those unblinking eyes, and it scared me as I had never been scared before.

Standing in front of the crowd were four Martians who, judging from the marks of respect given to them by the others, must have been leaders or dignitaries... They were pointing at us, uttering their strange sounds and making odd gestures, which were in turn echoed by the crowd.

"It looks like they're discussing our fate," said the Doctor.

"Maybe they're arguing about what sort of torture they're going to put us through," I replied gloomily.

"I don't think so. I'm almost certain they don't intend to kill us."

"How can you be sure?"

"I have... a certain facility for languages... Although I'll readily admit that these are among the strangest beings I've ever met... They seem to have both an individual consciousness and yet share in some form of collective mind... Most unusual..."

I looked at the Doctor to see if he was pulling my leg, but he seemed very serious. His eyes were squinting as he strained to hear what the creatures were saying.

"Besides, if they wanted to torture us, they'd already have done so, hmm?"

I had to admit to myself that the Doctor had a point. The Martians who appeared to be in charge seemed more curious than hostile or angry.

They now stepped towards us, cautiously, continuing their exchange of sharp noises and rapid gestures.

One of them reached towards the Doctor and, extending his long skeletal arm, touched our friend's head with his elongated fingers. They stayed like that, in silent communion, for a few seconds. The Doctor had closed his eyes. The Martian repeated three times something that, to me, sounded like:

"*Oyahu...Oyahu... Oyahu...*"

Then, he stepped back, waiting to see what would happen. He was not disappointed, for after opening his eyes, the Doctor slowly issued three words:

"*Oyahu... Zioa... Yao...*"

Whatever the Doctor had said, the effect on the crowd was prodigious.

The Martians rushed forward *en masse*, pushing the four leaders in front of them and almost squashing them against us.

I barely had time to become concerned by the surging of the crowd before orders were issued, and almost immediately, a metal barrier appeared between us and the crowd. How did they manage to erect it in such a record time?

They were masters of machines powered by invisible forces. I saw metal bars move seemingly of their own accord and assemble themselves into fences and posts. Even the unbreakable wire that had so invincibly held us prisoner was spun out like a spider's web by small, round spinnerets which popped out of the smooth metal like a bubble breaking the surface of a glass of milk.

These creatures were like the dwarves of our legends who commanded invisible spirits and made prodigious artifacts in their forges. I acquired a new respect for them, and came to the belief that no race that was so advanced could be hostile. Now, I realize my naivete, but then I knew no better.

I had reached that point in my reflections when I saw the crowd disperse as suddenly as a demonstration breaks down upon the arrival of the police. I also heard a low rustling sound, like that of a garden hose being dragged on the ground.

"What's that?" I asked the Doctor.

"Look."

"I don't see anything."

"Yes. Those platforms."

Now that he had directed my attention, I saw a large, flat silver tray gliding towards us, seemingly floating a foot or so off the ground. It kept advancing, showing no indication of stopping, like a deadly blade.

"By God! They're going to slice us in two!" said Fred.

"No, no, no," said the Doctor irritably. "These are obviously freight platforms, vehicles to transport us somewhere else."

The old scientist was right.

Once the platforms were a couple of feet away from us, they stopped instantly, without making any noise.

One of the leaders gathered a team of Martians, and began issuing new orders. Immediately, we were gripped by powerful metal arms that ended with three grapplers, not unlike those small implements we use to pick up sugar cubes.

I felt the wires loosen and vanish, as if they had evaporated around me. The metal arms grabbed me as if they were a human hand and deposited me on the platform. As soon as I lay on it, the binding wires returned, as if they had never left. It was incomprehensible.

The machines did the same with my two companions.

A few minutes later, I felt the platform zoom away, travelling faster and faster. Because I was lying on my back, I could see nothing except the pale, rosy sky above.

"Doctor? Doctor? Are you there?" I called.

But no voice answered me.

"Fred? Doctor? Where are you?" I screamed.

But I heard nothing except the whistle of the wind as we sped on.

I was alone at the mercy of the Martians.

Chapter Eight
Prisoners of the Martians

The hardship of my journey, and the weight of my emotions, had finally overcome me.

I had been slumbering, sleeping restlessly on and off, when I was suddenly awakened for good by great clanging sounds.

The platform on which I had been tied shifted rapidly in a zigzag pattern, as if it was a tray moved from hand to hand. Then I heard a whirring noise, and I felt myself being lowered into a shaft, almost as if I was inside an elevator.

The sky above me was now framed inside a rectangular window, which slowly shrunk in size, until it was closed down by a metal shutter.

'As long as I was still outside, I had irrationally preserved the hope that I might somehow be freed. But now that I was inside what looked like an underground building, I felt inescapably and irrevocably trapped. Whatever shred of courage I had earlier mustered had entirely abandoned me. I felt that the end had come.

The platform came to a sudden stop, and the metal wires which held me so tightly were slowly reabsorbed into the metal as ink into a blotter.

I sat up and looked around.

I stood in a square cell without doors. Its walls were made of smooth metal. They were crisscrossed by strange filaments of light, like veins embedded deeply inside their substance, that occasionally brightened with a blaze of purple fire. The shaft through which I had been lowered had closed above me, and I could see no trace of its opening in the convex ceiling above.

The air felt heavier than it did on the surface, where the atmosphere had been more rarefied. It contributed to my feelings of claustrophobia. I began to obsessively fear that the ceiling or the walls would come together and squash me, and even though I knew that this was unlikely, I could not shake that irrational dread.

Suddenly, one of the walls of my cell was drenched in purple light as the filaments inside it appeared to go wild...They flared up in strange geometric patterns, branching out until their tiny rivulets of fire covered its entire surface...

These strange lights must have changed the properties of the metal for it slowly became transparent. At first, I thought the entire wall was gone, but a push of my hand against it confirmed its existence. I was still a prisoner in my cell, like an animal in a zoo.

So that was to be my fate: being kept by the Martians as an object of curiosity!

On the other side of the glass wall, other lights slowly went up, and I saw that I was inside a vast underground cave. As I looked in horror, I saw Martians crawling down the rock walls like giant spiders. It was a horrible and fearsome sight.

They muttered words whose meanings I could not fathom.

"*Oyahu... Oyahu...*"

Four of them approached my cage–for I might as well call it that–and looked at me with curiosity, but no hostility as far as I could tell. I tried talking to them in my own language, but it was as if I had not spoken, for they paid no attention to me.

"*Lo hoo to zey,*" one of the gnomes finally said.

On that command, various metal blocks were extruded from the back wall of my cell, to make up places where I could sit, lie down and fulfill other natural functions.

Suddenly, the lights in the cavern brightened considerably. My four keepers turned around and. as I looked in the same direction as they, I saw a shiny purple mist appear in the distance.

Soon, two Martians stepped out of the mist, accompanied by a retinue of followers. These Martians were different from all the others we had seen before. They were taller, and while their bodies and limbs were just as frail-looking, their heads were much larger... rounder and bigger...

You may have seen cartoons representing a man with a pumpkinhead? Well, these Martians looked exactly like that. Pumpkinheads.

As they approached, I could see them better. Under any other circumstances, I might have been tempted to laugh at their appearance. But instead, I shrank back in fear, because somehow I knew that they would be the arbiters of my fate. These pumpkinheads were going to issue a verdict of life, death, or perpetual imprisonment. And there would be no appeal...

I decided to look humble, and waited apprehensively by the glass wall.

They stopped a few feet away from my cell, and looked at me. Their slit-like mouths opened and closed silently. They were still as a stone. I guessed that they had never seen an Earthman before, and were digesting the sight.

One of the two issued an order to a member of his entourage, and suddenly the two walls to the left and the right of me were crisscrossed with filaments of purple light and turned transparent.

I let out a scream of joy.

There, in the two cells next to mine, were the Doctor and Fred!

I was no longer alone!

We waved at each other in excitement, happy to be reunited, after a fashion. Though it became immediately apparent that we could not hear each other's words, no matter how loud we tried to shout, we whooped and cheered.

But the two Martians obviously could hear us, for they stepped back in panic at once. Some among their retinue even began to run away, until a sharp order from their bosses reminded them of their duty.

The Doctor had grasped the fact that, while we could not communicate with each other, it was possible for us to speak to our captors.

I saw him walk to the glass wall and utter a few words–which I presumed to be Martian language–to the two pumpkinheads.

They became thunderstruck to hear an alien being talk to them in their own tongue!

One of the two stepped closer. He was barely a yard away from our wall when a member of his retinue reminded him of their safety protocols (or so I presumed) and he stepped back a few paces.

Meanwhile, the Doctor continued addressing them. I could not hear what he said–and I would not have understood it in any event–but I could watch and hear the Martians' reactions.

The two leaders began actively conversing between themselves, occasionally reaching with their hands to touch each other's forehead, which I took to be a form of mental communication.

Finally, one of them turned towards the Doctor, and uttered a single word:

"*Vuitt?*" he said.

"*Vuitt*," nodded the Doctor.

The two pumpkinheads nodded back, and turning towards their entourage, issued a long string of instructions which, of course, I did not understand, except for a few recurring words such as *oyahu*, *zioa* and *razaiou*. The last word was repeated several times. Razaiou... *razaiou*...

Polite murmurs of approval greeted the speech. I was reminded of a university professor proffering his conclusions to his students, who in turn feel compelled to obsequiously agree with, and congratulate, the teacher for his superior mind.

The Martian "professors" departed gravely, followed by the entourage, and escorted by the other gnomes whom I had initially–and correctly–assumed to be our keepers.

"Well, at least they no longer think we're animals," I heard the Doctor say.

I turned towards the old scientist who was sitting calmly on a metal cube in his cell.

"Doctor! I can hear you!" I said.

"Me too," said Fred. "I can hear you both. Those dirty little gnomes have lifted their spell of silence."

"So you can actually speak to them? What did you say?" I asked Doctor Omega.

"The two Macrocephales we saw–it is an approximate translation of their title, and it means 'large heads'– were sent to determine whether we were some kind of unknown beasts or intelligent beings like them. They are familiar with the underwater reptile warriors and the other species we met on our journey. There is also apparently a race of little stone men in the southern hemisphere... But they do not consider any of these to be human beings, or perhaps I should say Martian beings, but merely animals, even though they have their own culture, their own civilization..."

"That's horrible!" I said.

The Doctor looked at me, his head slightly cocked, his cold, almost inhuman, stare suddenly back.

"Your own colonial empires do the same with respect to the native people of Africa and Asia, Borel. The human race is hardly in a position to criticize... Pray that it never suffers the fate that it so mercilessly imposes upon others..." Then his expression softened and he again became the wise old scientist I had come to love. "In any event, because I picked up a few words of their language, I was able to convince them that we, unlike those other groups, are worthy of being treated as equals..."

"So why are we still inside those rotten cages?" asked Fred.

"Would you let loose a Tartar or a Mohican in the streets of Paris, hmm? We may be intelligent beings like them, Fred, but that doesn't mean that they're not afraid of us. The Macrocephales are taking their findings back to those who will ultimately decide our fate... But I'm afraid I've got worse news to share with you, my friends..."

"Worse news?" I echoed stupidly, shuddering at the thought of what that might be.

"Yes. You two couldn't see it because you were tied down on the ground, and you were carried away by those flying platforms before I was. But, after they took you, and while I myself was being secured, the Martians from that factory used their machines to take apart the *Cosmos*..."

"Our ship is gone?"

"Not entirely. It's been disassembled. They had already taken apart most of the hull by the time they took me away... No doubt they wish to study it in their own laboratories... Not that I think they will understand its technology..."

I was reeling from the blow of learning that that wondrous craft that had required so much painstaking labor to put together and that had transported us successfully through the heavens was no more.

The inescapable conclusion was that the balance of our existence–assuming that the Martians did not decide to end our lives–would be spent on this inhospitable, alien world.

What life would we face on this strange planet where human laws did not apply, and where our needs and desires could find no legitimate outlet?

The Doctor had been right to compare our status to that of primitive tribesmen. I considered the dim prospect of being reduced to the level of an exotic native servant in some kind of Martian palace, or that of a local worker in a mine...

Worse, they might exhibit us in travelling sideshows like savages from another continent or monsters from a far-away isle... We would have to earn our food by doing tricks and meekly submitting to the wishes of our alien masters...

On Earth, our sorely missed homeworld, the very thought of which now filled my eyes with tears, we were citizens with rights, knowledge and responsibilities. On Mars, we knew nothing, could do nothing, and would inevitably be considered useless and odd-looking specimens.

I even feared that a more daring or a less compassionate Martian would want to dissect our bodies to further his knowledge of our anatomy and compare it with theirs. We would then end up becoming the subject of some academic dissertation, or stuffed artifacts in a zoological exhibit. I prayed that, at least, they would not vivisect us...

While I was absorbed in my gloomy reflections, Doctor Omega was pacing in his cell, walking in circles, obviously lost in deep thought. His eyes were hooded, and once in a while, he would snap his fingers, click with his tongue, or pull on his waistcoat, without paying attention to what Fred or I were doing.

I watched the old scientist as he ruminated his strange thoughts. I knew that I had little hope of comprehending them, for I had never met a man like him. Just looking at him gave me renewed hope that, perhaps, this amazing man would find a way to save us after all...

He was a genius. He could talk to the Martians. He could convince them to put the *Cosmos* back together, and to let us go... Nothing was beyond his abilities...

Feeling tired, I lay down and eventually drifted to sleep, feeling somewhat more hopeful.

By my reckoning, we remained prisoners in our cells for two more days, two more long and boring days...

Since our initial encounter with the Macrocephales, we had seen no more guards. No one had come to visit us, or even check up on us.

More importantly, no one had brought us any food.

We had begun to suffer from painful stomach cramps; at least, Fred and I did, for once again, Doctor Omega seemed better able than us to fight off the demands of the human body.

"Those savages are trying to starve us to death," said Fred.

"I don't think so," the Doctor replied. "We must be patient."

"But, Doctor, surely they're intelligent enough to realize that we need food, just like they do."

"Precisely, young man. Have you considered that their way of absorbing nourishment may be very different from ours, hmm? Maybe they eat only once a month, or..."

"Once a month!" screamed Fred. "We'll all be dead before then!"

"This was just an example, Fred. They probably eat very little, for they burn less energy..."

Our conversation was suddenly interrupted by the arrival of three Martians–ordinary Martians who looked just like our keepers–who crawled down the walls of the cavern like rats, and vanished into the darkness without paying us any attention.

We then heard a rumbling noise, as the platforms which had lowered us into our cells re-emerged from the metal floor. Above me, the rectangular opening in the ceiling slid open soundlessly.

One of the Martians reappeared and gestured us to climb on our respective platforms, also pointing at the opening in the ceiling.

I understood that, at long last, we were going to be freed, or at least taken to another accommodation. So, like my two friends, I stepped onto the platform eagerly and without hesitation.

It then continued its slow ascension towards the ceiling, and then up a metal shaft, until we finally saw the light of the day.

We had emerged into a great hall. We stood inside a divided section that was reminiscent of a court or an arena. On three sides, a crowd of excited Martians was staring at us with hundreds of reddish-yellow eyes glinting with curiosity, waving their skeletal arms and tentacle-like fingers.

There were also a few guards on each side, holding those deadly little boxes from which they had fired their painful red beams. Clearly, it was in our interest to be on our best behavior.

Before us, a committee of five Macrocephales stood on a metal dais that was perhaps four hundred square feet large. I guessed correctly that we were now going to be evaluated by a panel of judges or scientists.

The Doctor stepped towards the Macrocephales, and respectfully delivered a brief speech in the Martian language, which I cannot transcribe here.

The pumpkinheads seemed impressed, and began a heated exchange. Occasionally, one of the judges would touch another's head to communicate his thoughts more effectively. Once in a while, they threw glances at us. The crowd had grown silent, and I wondered what fate lay in store for us.

Finally, an old, wizened Macrocephale, who appeared to be their leader, made a sign and uttered a long, whistled command. Almost immediately, a small, frail-looking Martian was thrown into our arena. He looked extremely weak, even by their standards. You could tell that the poor creature was mortally afraid of us, for he was whining most horribly.

I looked at the Doctor questioningly.

"It's a test," he said. "They want to see that we're not blood-thirsty savages."

"By throwing one of their own to the wolves?" I exclaimed. "Isn't that the pot calling the kettle black?"

Meanwhile, the hapless Martian was trying to crawl away from us, but without much luck. The Doctor picked him up delicately and cradled him in his arms like a baby. He petted the creature's head as he would have done with a domestic cat or a small dog.

A buzz of sympathy began to emanate from the crowd.

The Doctor took this opportunity to say a few more words in Martian.

The old Macrocephale turned towards the rest of the judges and delivered a new speech. They conferred again, and after what seemed to me another heated debate, one of them came down from the dais and walked towards us.

That pumpkinhead did not appear to entirely trust us, but nevertheless managed to project a certain air of confidence as he approached. He knew that he was performing before the eyes of his superior and a large crowd of onlookers, and certainly did not want to appear cowardly. He strutted forward slowly, making little jumps. When he was only a few feet away, he stopped and addressed the Doctor.

"*Pohogo... Pohogo,*" he said in small, broken-sounding voice.

Still cradling the small Martian in his arms, the Doctor bowed his head, and repeated the same few words in Martian.

Then the Macrocephale became more daring. He made a small, almost frog-like jump forward, and with his long, tentacled fingers, reached forward to touch the old scientist. The Doctor smiled and with his free arm, also reached forward and let his finger rest on the Martian's enormous skull.

Screams of joy erupted around the room, as if they had just discovered a long-lost relative.

One after the other, the pumpkinheads descended from their dais and came to touch us and speak to us. It was obvious that they now accepted us as harmless, civilized beings.

They then sat again. With a gesture, the old Macrocephale dismissed the guards, probably in an effort to show that they, too, had no hostile intentions towards us. I was, of course, immensely relieved.

The Doctor put the small Martian down, and sat on the metal floor. We imitated him.

The little creature was no longer afraid of us, for it now stayed near us. Gaining in courage, he walked up to Fred and, after examining him with great concentration, gently pulled on his beard.

The big man laughed, and wishing to demonstrate his friendly intentions, gave a pat on the small Martian's head. However, our friend either did not fully understand his strength in this lower gravity, or underestimated the alien's frailness, for the gnome uttered at once a small painful cry.

Fred looked very contrite. The Doctor immediately took the little Martian in his arms again, and gently rubbed the top of his head.

The other Martians were very favorably impressed by this display of kindness, and cheered again. I could tell that they had gained a great deal of respect for Doctor Omega, who had impressed them with his science and gentility.

Another Macrocephale came towards me, presumably to take a closer look, and I bowed my head and extended my hand forward, as if I had been introduced to the Japanese emperor. When I now recall those scenes of our first interactions with the Martians, I can't help feeling both moved and amused at the same time. I think we would have looked very funny with our groping and pidgin human martian words to any visitor that might have seen us then.

One thing that puzzled my new friend were my clothes, which he felt, pulled at, all the time probably wondering what was that strange shell that covered my skin without sticking to it.

Acting upon the Doctor's suggestion, I got up and removed my jacket, my vest and my shirt, and stood before them bare-chested.

When at last the Martians saw my naked flesh, they were very surprised, as we would be, I suppose, if we saw a man taking off his own skin. But then the Macrocephale reached forth and touched me. The feeling of his cold, snake-like fingers on my body was initially strange, but not uncomfortable.

Meanwhile, the Doctor was working with their leader to enlarge his vocabulary and improve our abilities to communicate. They each had one hand on the other's head, while they were gesturing with the other. The Doctor would point to a part of his body, or items in the room, and the Martian would say the corresponding word. *Zao* was head, *crazao* arms, *ranai* chest, *piilit* legs, *clanoos* feet, and so forth...

Somehow, sitting next to the Doctor, I–more quickly than Fred, I will say–soon acquired a rudimentary understanding of the language, which I transcribed in my notebooks, after repeating each word and making sure that I had gotten their exact phonetics.

The Macrocephales were visibly amazed by the Doctor's ability to start building complex sentences, while my improvised dictionary was growing at an astonishing pace.

Meanwhile, Fred was again starting to grumble loudly. After all, we had not eaten in several days, and only the excitement of the last few hours had managed to make me forget the pangs of hunger.

Trying to communicate through gestures, the big man made the well-recognized motion of opening his mouth and chewing, while using his right hand to mime bringing invisible food to his mouth. Needless to say, the Martians did not understand what he wanted and just looked at him with curiosity.

The Doctor and I smiled at seeing Fred's discomfited expression.

"Unlike the less evolved Martians we met in the North," said the Doctor, "these have no teeth, as you can tell from their mouths. I doubt they masticate their food. It must be ingested in liquid form...."

"Can you ask them for food?" I said. "I'm starving too. And thirsty."

"Yeah. If I don't get some food soon, I'm going to eat one of them Martians!" said Fred. And from the look on his face, I was inclined to take his threat seriously.

"Wait," said the Doctor. "Don't do anything stupid. I'm going to try asking for food..."

The Doctor launched himself in a small speech, of which I understood very little in spite of my dictionary, except that I thought that, at one point, he got bogged down explaining the concept of eating animals, which was clearly incomprehensible to our hosts.

But finally, they understood him, for the leader of the Macrocephales uttered an order and very quickly four Martians returned with a small table that moved without friction across the metal floor.

"*Babaio*," said the Macrocephale.

He removed the glass top that covered the table and we saw a number of small colored balls just like the glass marbles with which children play.

"*Babaio*," said the Macrocephale again, taking one of the balls and swallowing it.

"Nutrition pills, of course," said the Doctor. "I should have guessed. Let me try one..."

He took a pill, put it in his mouth, then after a few seconds, swallowed it.

"They're excellent and totally safe. Go ahead..."

Fred and I reached into the table and gobbled a couple of pills each. Our feeling of hunger disappeared instantly, but we still felt horribly thirsty.

The Martian, somehow anticipating our thoughts, slid another compartment open, revealing thin yellow strips that looked like wax. We each slipped two in our mouths, and the most miraculous thing happened. Our thirst was quenched immediately... Our palate felt a wondrous sensation of freshness as I had never experienced before... It was truly incredible...

Fred's stupefaction was evidently displayed on his face... As for the Doctor, he looked admiringly at the display of pills before us.

"These Martians are astonishing... amazing... full of surprises!" he exclaimed.

After we had finished our meal, the leader of the Macrocephales issued a series of orders filled with strange new words I did not recognize.

The dais sank back into the floor without a trace and the metal wall behind it slid open silently. Some Martians in the crowd tried to use this opportunity to come and see us closer, but the Macrocephale would have none of it. He signaled to the guards, who had returned with their devilish little boxes, and they kept the throng at bay.

"What's inside those boxes?" I asked the Doctor, still massaging the spot on my hand where their rays had burned me.

"Radium, I think... Its disintegration is caused by its interaction with a radiation still unknown to your scientists, that propagates throughout the Universe... My theory is that the box shields the radium inside from that radiation and hence makes it possible to stimulate it into explosive transmutation..."

"Really?" I said, badly feigning understanding.

"Perhaps... I'll know for certain soon enough..." replied the old scientist with that manic gleam in his eyes that augured the anticipation of new discoveries.

Meanwhile, an egg-shaped metal vehicle had glided silently into the hall. It seemed supported by two cylinders affixed perpendicularly to its axis on the bottom, except of course that they did not touch the ground. If it was powered by an engine, I could see no trace of it, since it was almost entirely hollowed out to make room for its passengers.

The Macrocephales entered the ovoid and invited us to follow them inside. The top of the vehicle was reabsorbed into its substance to make room for Fred, who was taller than two of the Martians together.

When we were all settled in, one of the Martians touched a spot on the inside wall and the ovoid took off at rapid speed.

In spite of its pace, I was able to at last see where we were: in a vast city made up of metal buildings. They were all of the same silver grey color, but came in many disconcerting shapes. Some were cones, others truncated pyramids, needles, domes, discoids, or even convex copulas. Many were taller than anything I had seen in Paris or London, and rivaled the famous skyscrapers of New York.

A blue mist hung over the landscape, distorting it and giving it a strange, dream-like quality.

Once in a while, other vehicles whizzed by, above or next to us. Some were people transports like ours; others were large platforms, such as the one which had carried us earlier, and contained goods and raw materials.

After a while, we left the city. Our acceleration increased to even more vertiginous speed as we crossed a desolate plain, the only features of which were canals and tall, vertical silver trees with drooping branches.

Then I saw that we were approaching another city, which quickly filled our horizon. It looked like a powerful citadel made of black metal, surrounded by reddish clouds. It was a fearsome sight to behold.

"*Razaiou... razaiou...*" said our companions, shaking their heads in cadence.

"*Razaiou*?" I asked the Doctor, not understanding that word even though this was not the first time I had heard it.

"Their supreme leader, I think," said the Doctor. "They're taking us to see their King..."

The ovoid stopped just as we reached the city. Before us was a raging torrent; only it was not a torrent of water but of some mysterious molten metal from which rose billows of acrid smoke.

One of the Macrocephales activated another hidden switch and from somewhere within the citadel, a metal arm extended and extruded cables which grabbed our vehicle and lifted it in the air above the smoking torrent with astonishing strength.

I had personally experienced the deceptive strength of these thin Martian cables, and therefore I was not surprised to see our ovoid being carried like a dirigible hundreds of feet in the air and deposited onto another metal ramp that plunged into the bowels of the citadel.

"These Martian are remarkable engineers," marveled the Doctor. "Their metallurgic technology is without peer... I've never seen anything like it...Such precision, such delicacy... Look, now we're travelling down..."

Indeed, we were now sliding rapidly alongside a network of shiny metal ramps that crisscrossed the interior of that formidable city. I saw other vehicles such as ours hurrying on mysterious errands. This was evidently a seat of power. If the Martians had a capital, we had definitely come to it.

The Doctor shared my thoughts for he said with renewed enthusiasm:

"We have every reason to hope, my friends, that the masters of this fantastic city will let me reassemble our dear *Cosmos*..."

Our vehicle finally arrived before another, even more colossal building. I expected it to be grabbed by another hauling system, but instead the ovoid shot up an almost vertical ramp at full speed and reached its top effortlessly.

It was a prodigious palace. Its metal towers and domes stood starkly contoured against the red sky. Its massive gates were ornately decorated with metal carvings of various Martian symbols that looked like clubs and fleur-de-lis.

These slid upwards like the curtains of a theater as our vehicle entered.

We eventually stopped in a trapezoid-shaped courtyard. I saw garlands of shiny stones that ran alongside the walls, and decorations made of a strange metal, the color of which seemed to shift when you looked at it.

We were greeted by two rows of Martians who immediately stood at attention against the walls, shaking little bells that produced a muffled ringing.

The Macrocephales got off the ovoid and invited us to follow them.

Accompanied by an enthusiastic crowd, we entered the palace of the *Great Razaiou*.

Chapter Nine
Guests of the Great Razaiou

After crossing a series of long hallways adorned with bizarre metal artifacts, we were led into a vast hall, a description of which I find almost impossible to write, so extravagant and complex were its decoration.

A throne made of some kind of blue metal, located under a cupola of red glass, stood upon a dais in an alcove embellished with stones that might have been rubies or topaz.

It was indeed a throne fit for a King–likely that of the Great Razaiou before whom we were going to appear...

I don't mind admitting that I felt apprehensive at that moment. How would the leader of the Martians greet us?

Would he reveal himself to be an enlightened monarch, or a mere brute with a crown on his head?

Suddenly, I heard the nasal sound of trumpets; the lights came on in the room, and the King made his entrance.

He was not very different from the other Macrocephales whom we had met, except that his head may have been slightly larger and his body older and more decrepit. The image of a pumpkin sitting on top of a stick-like insect body again crossed my mind.

This Master of Mars, however, wore a complicated, cone-like tiara on his head, and in his right hand, gripped a small metal rod, the tip of which was a crystal that radiated a soft blue light. I had no doubt that this scepter could become a very effective weapon if necessary.

He wore a necklace of yellow stones around his neck, and a square-shaped medallion which, as I later found, contained a portrait of his beloved queen. This detail showed that, notwithstanding the great cosmic distances we had travelled, certain things remained the same throughout the universe...

The Great Razaiou entered from the back of the hall, sitting on top of a small floating disk that deposited him on his throne. As he prepared to see us, all the Martians in the room lay on the floor, flat on their backs, and hit the ground repeatedly with their heads saying *"razaiou, razaiou"* like a prayer sung in unison.

We, on the other hand, chose to remain standing, in a posture showing respect, but without trying to mimic that peculiar salute.

Once installed on his throne, the Razaiou waved his scepter and two of the Macrocephales approached him, their heads slightly tilted back, and the tentacled fingers of their left hand on their throat, which I assumed was a token gesture of submission, like our removing our hats or bowing our heads on Earth.

When they stood before the throne, they each spun around twice like a top, then waited for a command from their master.

The Razaiou made another gesture, and the first Macrocephale began talking. Although I actually under- stood very little of his long speech, I was able to figure out that it was a report of our discovery, our capture, our imprisonment, and what we had undergone until now.

After the report was ended, the King mulled it over in silence for what seemed to me a very long time. Then he began talking to us in a frail, monotone voice, like that of a very old man. When I said that he was talking to us, I mean to say that he was, in fact, addressing Doctor Omega, who had been described to him as the most fluent in their language.

So our amazing friend was the first man to have the honor of being presented to Martian royalty!

This time, the Doctor decided to comply with the rules of local etiquette. He approached the throne his head slightly tilted back and his left hand on his throat. He then pirouetted twice, and waited under the King's benevolent eyes.

I was next to be introduced... I mimicked the Doctor without any trouble... Not so our friend Fred, however... The big man almost lost his balance and would have fallen against the royal personage had I not caught him. The Razaiou appeared fearful, but the Doctor smoothed over the incident with a few well-chosen words.

I was again asked to take off my garments. When the Razaiou saw my naked chest, he touched me with his scepter, and seemed surprised by my softness. He smiled and shook his head, pointing at his own chest and explaining that he, too, had clothes "made of skin, but harder."

He then examined the Doctor's head, his slick white hair, and his shiny, ivory forehead. He placed his fingers against the scientist's head, and they began to communicate in that strange mix of words and mental pictures.

I now recognized a fair number of Martian words, but unlike the Doctor, I had difficulty in assembling them into coherent sentences. However, my musical training was useful, for I had a good ear for sounds, and was able to speak without accent, which was important since the Martian language, like Japanese on Earth, placed a great deal of value on specific intonations.

For example, the word *gho* meant tree, nose, eye or knee, depending on how one pronounced it. Being able to project a mental picture directly into the mind of one's interlocutor greatly facilitated conversations. But while the Doctor was obviously skilled at such form of communication, both Fred and I were hopeless. Our large friend could only utter noises that sounded like a cross between the cooing of a pigeon and the baa-ing of goats, but nothing that sounded like Martian. His pidgin Martian later became a constant source of amusement for our hosts.

In order to pin down the exact meaning of the Martian words, I had drawn on my notebook a musical scale where I recorded a word, not only phonetically but with the musical notes that corresponded to this or that meaning.

The Doctor had diplomatically conveyed to the Razaiou the pleasure that we three felt in being granted an audience by the greatest brain of Mars. (The actual word was not "brain" but *molokô* which described both an advanced state of erudition and wisdom and the physical organ that contained such a state.)

He also assured him that we were mere explorers seeking to discover new lands and new people, and that they had nothing to fear from us...

That speech was visibly much appreciated by the King, who replied:

"I see now that you are indeed intelligent animals... Far more intelligent than the *Setissi*..."

The word "animal" only meant that we were not of their race and was not to be taken as an insult... As to the word *Setissi*, I later understood that it referred to the underwater reptilian race, with whom the Razaiou's race had been at war for thousands of years.

"Is it true that you come from the Blue Star that we see in the evening sky?" asked the King.

I had indeed noticed during our journey across the plains of Mars that the fourth planet had different morning and evening stars than Earth's Venus. This Martian star was bright enough to cast shadows, and shone like a blue-white jewel in the Martian sky. It was our homeworld: Earth.

We learned that the Razaiou's predecessors had long tried to communicate with Earth, sending huge beams of light in the skies, trying to catch our attention, hoping for a response. Alas, this was the Earth of billions of years ago, and there was none to answer them.

They had finally abandoned their efforts. We were separated by more than a gulf of space, but also by a gulf of time...

When the Doctor explained how we had travelled to Mars, the King's eyes grew wider, and became quite enthused, even though I realized later that he had little scientific education, and understood almost nothing of even the simplest of the Doctor's explanations.

He was even more amazed to discover that I was forty years old, and that on Earth, as a general rule, people died in their eighties or nineties.

The Macrocephales, by contrast, enjoyed a prodigious longevity... Their average life span was three hundred...

During the first couple of hundred years, they were *vizado*, which meant both adult and active; they then became *gayado*, which meant both retired and inactive, even of diminished capacity... I was told that the *gayado* lived in cities where they ended their days peacefully, served by the *noussaï*, which was the name given to the working class Martians with smaller heads that we had met at the factory.

The Great Razaiou himself was 157 years old, but his queen Bilitii was only five... Surprisingly, the Martians did not experience childhood or adolescence. Only a few weeks after his birth, a Martian reached his full-grown state. The mind acquired more knowledge and life experience, but the body remained substantially the same...

After asking us at some length about the political and economic organization of Earth, the Razaiou began displaying some signs of tiredness. He gave us leave to go, after telling us that we were now free to go where we wished in his Kingdom, and ordering his subjects to treat us with the greatest respect.

He then leaned back on his throne and fell asleep. Our audience was over.

The two Macrocephales said they would take us to our apartments, and escorted us out of the great hall and into a large garden where we were surprised to discover yet one more type of Martian, different from all those we had seen before.

These had heads that were more pointy, more oval than spherical, and their skin was markedly more yellow than green. Their eyes were slanted, their mouths smaller, and they sported a bud of a nose instead of slits. They were dressed in togas made of multi-colored crystals that shined and sparkled as they moved.

As we approached a group of these new Martians, they spotted us and uttered a series of high-pitched cries. Some even ran away.

Our guides quickly reassured them, and they began to look at us with less fear and suspicion.

In a corner of the garden, there was an area covered with vines that had thorns like our cacti...

With decorum and ceremony, the Macrocephales took us there to introduce us to another important personage. Three new Martians sat there, one sporting a headdress reminiscent of the Great Razaiou's.

"I understand now!" I told my companions. "It's the Queen! These are female Martians!"

"Bilitii," said one of our escorts, confirming my guess, before lying on the ground and displaying the usual marks of respect.

Perhaps because of her young age, Queen Bilitii was obviously far more impressionable than her husband. The sight of what must have been to her three hairy giants with pink skin and grimacing faces, was too much to bear.

After a couple of polite words, she gathered her ladies and left. We were neither particularly surprised, nor offended by her reaction. I remembered the reaction of the little queen of Mildendo when she first cast eyes on Gulliver...

However, our guides seemed genuinely chagrined that we had not been treated with more civility, and endeavored to show us more of the natural beauties that surrounded the palace...

First, they took us to a park filled with tall red flowers and those trees which seemed to be made of marble that we had seen during our journey. It was pleasantly shaded and very beautiful.

We saw strange-looking birds with curved beaks, jagged wings and long, stilt-like legs that hopped or flew around, uttering piercing little cries. They would occasionally twist madly upon themselves like tops, then collapse on the ground, before getting up, seemingly no worse for the wear.

A little further on, we saw a new animal that looked like a large cucumber with six feet. They moved quickly and one of them even jumped at me, causing me to fall on my back. The Macrocephales were much amused; I learned that these were harmless pets.

Then, I saw something slithering in the grass that made me recoil in horror.

Small, black snakes, thin as eels, hairy like caterpillars.

I already wrote about my feelings of repulsion towards snakes, so I need not restate them here. As soon as I saw the reptiles crawl towards me, I jumped up in the air as if I had stepped on live coals.

I thought I read an expression of pity—as much as one could read anything there—on the faces of the Macrocephales.

Obviously, they could not understand why I felt the way I did towards these animals which they treated as pets, cradling them in their hands, letting them slither all over their bodies. Two reptiles had slid up the Doctor's legs and one of them was already perched high on his shoulder.

"Doctor! How can you let those awful beasts climb all over you?" I said in horror.

"They aren't awful, Borel!" he replied. "These snakes are sacred animals, like cats were to the ancient Egyptians or cows are to the Hindus.... Learn to overcome your fears... Be more tolerant... And also remember that if you kill one, you run the risk of angering our hosts..." he added with a sadistic smile, having once again anticipated my thoughts.

"They're not all that different from grass snakes, except for that hair," remarked Fred, who had grabbed one of the snakes and was looking at it.

I resigned myself to not squash any of the snakes under my heel and repressed a shudder as I let one climb on my shoes.

It was a mistake, as I immediately discovered when the foul beast stung me in the leg with its single fang!

I screamed in pain, and tore away the wretched snake and hurled it to the ground.

The two Macrocephales who escorted us immediately rushed towards me. One rubbed my wound with the tip of his tentacled finger and, almost as if by miracle, all sensations of burning and pain vanished. The other one was similarly ministering to the snake.

As one can surmise, the incident had cast a pall on the visit to the gardens, and we were then rushed to our quarters and left alone to rest.

We had been assigned three spacious rooms, contiguous to each other, with doorway-like entrances but no doors. The Doctor theorized that one could seal the rooms by summoning some kind of invisible curtain.

Each room was furnished only with a low bed that was completely square. There were no table or chairs, or any decorative items, except for a square window-like screen built into a wall that Doctor Omega was unable to turn on–he claimed that it was some communication device–in spite of all his efforts.

We were all very tired after the events of the day; so we each retired to our rooms and quickly fell asleep on our beds.

In the morning, soon after we woke up, several Martian gnomes, of the *noussaï* category, came and brought us nutrition pills and tablets of various sizes and colors with an amiability which I found slightly disturbing.

The Doctor appeared to be his usual unflappable, confident self, but I was a little concerned. While we were apparently being treated nicely, I still could not fathom the Macrocephales' true intentions towards us. And we had made no progress towards getting our ship back together...

When I shared these concerns with the Doctor, he just shrugged them off.

"You're being far too suspicious, young man," he said. "The Martians have no reason to wish us ill. We're of too much interest to them for that... Stop worrying... I'm totally confident that I'll soon be able to embark on reassembling our ship."

"But you said you saw them take it apart... What if they damaged it? What if you can't put it back together?"

"They were being very careful... No doubt that when I find out where they took it... Probably a laboratory of some kind to study its workings... I'll be able to get it working again..."

The Doctor told me that he was eager to complete his learning of the Martian language, especially its scientific and technical terms, in order to petition the Great Razaiou to give him access to the ship, and the manpower necessary to put it back together...

He explained to me, patiently, as one would explain things to a child, that ultimately the Martians would want us to leave, and therefore they would have no reason to cripple his efforts.

I was only partially reassured by my friend's logic, but I saw no other course of action to follow.

The next few days went by without any great changes. We were treated very nicely by our staff–I had come to think of them that way–which continued to bring us nutrition pills.

Fred began to put on some serious weight, looking even more massive than usual. He could no longer button his pants, and had to use a makeshift belt to hold them up.

The Doctor warned him that, when the *Cosmos* was ready to take off, any extra weight might make our leaving more difficult. That warning did not go unheeded, and thereafter Fred consumed fewer pills.

He and I even embarked upon an exercise program!

Each day, we walked for two hours, the equivalent of roughly going around the gardens fifty times. Our staff looked upon this feat, which to them was truly Herculean, with awe, and we began to garner a little coterie of watchers who would come to see the "big aliens" (or *Babazeio*, which was the term they used to refer to

us) run around the garden so many times without stopping or collapsing.

By then, I had started to become increasingly fluent
in Martian, although not as much as the Doctor, who was
now absorbed in the study of their books, or rather their
cylinders, since they stored information on long sheets
of shiny foil-like paper rolled into tube-shaped contain-
ers.

The Macrocephales had also brought us tablets in-
scribed with their cuneiform-like script which, I gather,
were the equivalent of alphabet books or children's
learning aids on their planet. The characters reminded
me vaguely of those of Ancient Mesopotamia. As I
mentioned, the Martian language was made up of a
combination of guttural and sing-song syllables, and
mastering the exact intonation was essential.

Because of my musical skills, I soon became more
adept at it than even the Doctor. My old friend helped
me with my spelling, however, an area in which I
showed far less competence than he, by using a brush
dipped into a green, rubbery ink to record with amazing
ease even the most complex sequences of cuneiform
signs in my notebook.

We thus spent four weeks as guests of the Great
Razaiou, learning Martian science and culture, being
treated like honored visitors (*garagoulô*). We were
granted more audiences with the King, during which we
discussed other aspects of life on Earth and on Mars.

As would be the case on Earth, being this close to
the King made our company desirable, and all the Martians who were important made a point of meeting us at
least once, so our social calendar quickly became very
crowded. Not to put a fine point on it, we had become
the toast of Martian High Society.

A kind of electric car (*plooplô*) with a chauffeur had been placed at our disposal by the Razaiou and we could go wherever we wished in the capital, which I had since learned was called Musiolii.

Every place we went, we were mobbed by throngs of curious Martians who had come to see the *Babazeio*. The only incident occurred when we were pressed against such a crowd that Fred unwittingly stepped on a Martian's foot, crushing it entirely.

Strangely, no one seemed to particularly mind... Martians were not as emotional as we humans are, and such an injury was deemed rather insignificant... especially since it had been inflicted without malice on a member of one of the less fortunate classes...

In the meantime, Doctor Omega had finally broached, to the Great Razaiou, the subject of letting him start working on putting the *Cosmos* back together. As my friend had guessed, the Martians did not intend to keep us prisoner forever and the King had happily granted his permission.

The Doctor had been so eager to visit the Macrocephales' scientific cities that he was like a child going to a candy store the fateful day when we received the authorization to proceed.

The Martians took us to an industrial complex called *Giiloz*, which may or may not have been the same place where we had been captured, but looked virtually indistinguishable to me. It reminded me of our great steel city of Le Creusot in the sense that it was entirely devoted to scientific and industrial work.

As we embarked upon a guided tour, we marveled at the Martians' technical ingenuity.

There were legions of workers employed in those factories... In one place, I saw perhaps more than five thousand of them...

And all those little men worked with surprising industry.

With their tentacled fingers, they controlled powerful machines which, in turn, controlled ever more powerful machines, of such complexity that my mind could not even fathom their workings.

Being weak of body, the Martians had created a technology that more than compensated for their lack of strength.

Electricity and magnetism, the use of which was still relatively rare on Earth, reigned supreme here. I saw huge blocks of metal floating smoothly on magnetic conveyor belts and thrown into vast machines were they were flattened in a few seconds by invisible forces.

Thanks to their mastery over the mighty energies of nature, the Martians powered thousands of machines and transported and reshaped hundreds of tons of raw metals. Pistons moved up and down, valves opened and shut, wheels turned, other complicated parts slid, rotated, rose, thrusted, pushed, all with a ballet-like precision of control and movement that seemed unimaginable.

I thought of a gigantic pocket watch inside which every cog and spring worked harmoniously together to create a greater harmony with a single purpose...

With little effort, the Martians were building marvels worthy of giants.

The industrial complex in which we were was specialized in the production of moving vehicles, which was why the *Cosmos*, or rather its parts, had been sent here for study. We were also shown another factory that similarly produced houses, or rather metal dwellings, using the same prodigious technology.

On Mars, everything was made of metal, and could be assembled or disassembled in a matter of minutes, which explained the fate that had befallen our ship...

I then understood that, to the Martians, housing and transportation were one and the same!

All their cities were mobile and could be moved at will. The reason for such feats was simple: During the summer (*zonartiz*), some areas became too hot and those cities were then moved northward.

For a few days every year, a prodigious migration took place during which Martian cities moved north before the summer, and south before the advent of winter.

Only the industrial cities remained on the spots where they were built, but these were equipped with temperature controls that enabled the workers to continue their labors in tolerable conditions. In any event, I had soon gathered that the improvement of the workers' condition was not of great concern to the ruling Macrocephale elite.

In Martian society, every individual was assigned a very precise position in life, and remained at that position until his death. Even to the point of being assigned a specific task, such as controlling this machine or that machine.

Intelligence mattered little in the handling of the machines which had been designed by the Macrocephales to be fool-proof. As long as a worker did his job correctly, the system worked in a flawless fashion. Indeed, I was told that there were almost never any industrial accidents, as is sadly the case on Earth.

The society was comprised of four classes: the ruling Macrocephales, who were the scientists and engineers, the *noussaï* or *giiloï*, the former being workers on the cities, the latter workers from the factories, both of which we were acquainted with, the *bafouro* or farm laborers, who were in charge of agriculture and food production, and finally the *gayado* or the retired, which I mentioned earlier.

Food production was of the highest importance since all Martians were vegetarians. In fact, I soon realized that more energy and resources were spent on agriculture on Mars than even in my native France!

The Martian wheat is something that they called *postoûm* which meant "red grass," because of its color, and which was the basis for most of their alimentation. *Postoûm* produced conical ears not unlike those of corn which, once ground, gave a tasty yellow powder called *postoûmi*.

Postoûmi was the main ingredient of the nutrition pills and tablets which we consumed. It surprised me to learn that to make a single two-gram tablet required nearly thirty kilograms of *postoûmi*. The powder was first left exposed to the air for two days, then baked in ovens. The result produced a highly concentrated food substance. A variety of tastes was obtained by the addition of *tililas* (a kind of blue pepper), *mouzaia* (salt, as far as I could determine), but most of the flavored pills were made for the Macrocephales, the rest of the population being given unflavored or raw *postoûmi*.

There were a few animals, such as the snakes which we had seen, which were kept primarily as pets and were fed with leaves of *smaia*, a cactus-like plant.

Doctor Omega, of course, radiated with joy since he had been granted the permission to visit *Giiloz* and interface with its Martian scientists and engineers. He spent his entire days there, returning home in the evening with bits and pieces of metal and various components the purpose of which I could not even imagine.

He had asked for, and obtained, a metal table and a chair that he used as a work bench in his room... I kept wondering what he intended to do with these pieces of machinery, but he always found a way to avoid answering my questions...

In the meantime, we had been able to view the *Cosmos* again... Our craft had indeed been taken apart by the Martian workers, but according to the Doctor, it was materially undamaged...

With the permission of the Great Razaiou, a special Martian factory dubbed *Büttowanohaz* (meaning "alien craft metallic reassembly project") had been set up just for that purpose.

The Macrocephale in charge of the project was a scientist named Tiziraou, who had already questioned the Doctor as to the ship's propulsion methods, vaguely hoping to understand its technology.

Unlike virtually all the other Martians we had met, Tiziraou exhibited a genuine curiosity towards our craft. He and the Doctor spent endless hours discussing the chemical composition of *stellite*, which was beyond the Macrocephale's understanding. To him, that substance was both a metal and not-a-metal, and that fact puzzled him greatly.

Tiziraou ran a great many tests to try to fathom its nature, but it was a metal so different from everything else he knew that he could not grasp its essence.

The Doctor, I suspect, contributed to his ignorance by offering them a series of explanations and scientific equations which were likely to send him on a scientific wild goose's chase.

As to the *temporal rotor* and the *vector generator*, which had successfully guided our ship to that ancient era, fortunately, both components had been carefully preserved and stored. The Doctor was satisfied that nothing would prevent their proper reinstallation once the ship was finished.

Because these two machines had nothing to do with metallurgy, the Martian scientists had ignored them and seemed to be oddly indifferent to them, as I suppose a French scientist may be indifferent to a Tibetan prayer wheel. Only Tiziraou exhibited any interest at all in their functions.

The Doctor, hoping to get our ship back together quickly, was cooperating with the Martians by drawing schematics with a stylus on those sheets of foil-like paper. Once in a while, he left his work to go and take a leisurely walk in the gardens, but soon returned to his work table.

It took the amazing old man two weeks to reconstruct, entirely from memory, the diagrams and schematics that he had once shown me that fateful evening in his wood-paneled study in Normandy.

He covered ten large metal tablets with complex etchings, cut-away diagrams, graphs, and all kinds of squiggles that must have meant something to the Martian engineers but that were totally incomprehensible to me.

I was astonished by how little time it took Tiziraou and his colleagues to understand the Doctor's work. The Martian scientist was even able to immediately complete or rectify a line that had been carelessly drawn in one of the schematics. These Martians were born engineers!

Nothing that had to do with metal strength, alloys and their chemical composition, design equations, insulation and manufacturing was foreign to them. They even made worthwhile suggestions as to how improve certain aspects of our craft. They replaced our clumsy electric generators with a much smaller and far more efficient engine that had an output of nearly three hundred fifty horsepower.

Martian metal workers who were in truth no bigger than hares and black as crows replaced our gears and most of the mechanical parts, such as the propeller and the tracks, with better engineered and more durable equivalents.

Finally, they used a special transparent metallic crystal which they called *Onozitis*, which had all the properties of glass but was virtually unbreakable, to replace our portholes, carefully lifting and applying the thin layer of stellite to the shiny new substance.

I could tell that some of these improvements mildly irritated the Doctor, who was very proud of his own engineering skills, but he wisely kept his own counsel this time.

The work was proceeding apace, and our craft was being recreated under our very eyes, as I had first seen it done in Le Creusot those many months ago, when suddenly something happened that almost meant the end of our efforts.

War had broken out on Mars!

Chapter Ten
War on Mars

First, I have to begin by telling you what happened that fateful morning, and how the story of our adventure on Mars thereafter took a turn for the worst...

We had taken the electric car placed at our disposal to travel as usual to the *Büttowanohaz* to check on the progress of reassembling the *Cosmos*. Unusually, however, perhaps moved by some mysterious instinct, both Fred and I had decided to accompany Doctor Omega...

When we reached the factory, we experienced the surprise of our lives: our ship was missing. It was no longer in its berth, which sat empty.

The Martians had moved it, but where?

We began searching for the *Cosmos*, looking for Tiziraou or any of his colleagues–they alone would have the answers to our questions. But the factory was strangely deserted, and the little workers either scurried away when they saw us or just plain ignored us.

For well over an hour, Fred and I climbed scaffoldings, walked down metal shafts, explored twisted networks of pipes and tubes, looked inside cage-like structures hanging in midair searching for an engineer to talk to, but all in vain.

"What do you think happened?" I finally asked the Doctor.

"I don't know. It's all very strange," he replied, frowning.

"You don't think that King of theirs got it moved to his personal museum?" asked Fred.

I immediately pictured our wonderful machine displayed on a stand like an antique Roman chariot in a museum, with a sign telling the visitors to not touch the exhibit. ("*Coaia bo ua tomaiozo*," I could not help thinking in Martian.)

"I don't think so," said the old scientist. "They wouldn't have spent so much time restoring it to its functionality if that had been their intention to begin with. No, there must be something else, but what?"

"The little workers seemed more agitated than usual," I observed. "I noticed they blinked their eyes very fast at me, like panicked animals..."

"Hmm... I suggest we return to the city... If our hosts want us, it'll be easier for them to find us there..."

Having no other sensible alternative to suggest, I agreed with the Doctor and we made the journey back, wondering all the time if we would ever see our beloved *Cosmos* again.

As we approached our quarters, Doctor Omega was again proven right, for I saw that Tiziraou, Loziou and

Boulanoi, the two Macrocephales who had been assigned to us by the Great Razaiou, were waiting for us.

I could tell right away that they, too, were in an agitated state...

We learned the grim news almost immediately.

The Southern Martians, or Southrons, had declared war on the Great Razaiou's Northern Martians. In fact, the invasion had already begun and the North was presently under attack.

The reason for the conflict was as old as time itself. The Southrons merely wanted to enlarge their territory in order to gain control of more arable land, harvest more *postoûm*, and produce more nutrition pills. I could see that this was a very grave matter, and that the specter of starvation loomed large in the Macrocephales' minds.

The Great Razaiou, we were told, had been anticipating an invasion for quite some time. The aggressive way in which we had initially been met when we had entered the industrial complex was but a reflection of the preparation of his people for the hard times ahead.

The Martians had also been stockpiling food and weapons in massive arsenals.

"The Great Razaiou has asked us to convey you to the palace most urgently," said Loziou in his sing-song voice.

We inquired about the location of the *Cosmos*, but were told only that the Great Razaiou wanted to see us and would answer all our questions, so we followed the three Macrocephales.

Outside, the city appeared to be the subject of an unusually high level of activity. Strange vehicles, of a kind that I had not seen before, buzzed around on the speedways. They carried squadrons of *noussaï*, *giiloï*, and even *bafouro*, all equipped with the same type of little box that had reminded me of a Kodak brownie camera and which I knew was capable of projecting a burning red beam, but larger. I assumed they were like soldiers being dispatched to the front, a guess which was indeed confirmed by one of our guides.

Macrocephale officers were ordering foot soldiers around, and all their orders were immediately obeyed... There was much agitation everywhere, and the city itself quaked and rumbled with the preparations for war...

We were ushered into the palace, and quickly admitted to the presence of the Great Razaiou.

The King of the Northern Martians filled us in briefly on the extent and gravity of the situation, before finally saying that he had read the daily reports about our craft that were sent to him, and that he wanted us to join him on the battlefield.

To say that our jaws dropped would be an understatement!

"Out of the question!" said the Doctor. "We're here on a mission of peace. We're not involved in your wars. My ship is not a weapon, it is a..."

The Doctor was groping for a word, and I suggested *mayoclei*, which was the nearest thing the Martians had to a flying car but one used for leisurely excursions. The Earth equivalent would have been to state that the *Cosmos* was not a battleship but a pleasure yacht.

The Great Razaiou, to his credit, tried a modicum of flattery, genuinely attempting to enlist our cooperation. He said that he would be happy to have us at his side during the coming hostilities... That we and our magnificent ship would be of great assistance... That it would repay their hospitality a thousandfold...

The Doctor could not have cared less, but this is one time where I think my instincts were more in tune with the situation than his. I had no doubt in my mind that if we did not agree with the monarch, he would stop asking–and just seize our ship or worse.

I stepped into the conversation, and begged the Great Razaiou to let me confer with my friends. I then took the Doctor and Fred aside, although I doubted the Martians could understand our words even if they heard them.

"Doctor, I fear we haven't got any choice," I said.

"You're mistaken, young man," he replied rather tetchily. "We always have a choice. We could leave. Our ship is virtually ready. I need only to reconnect the *temporal rotor* and..."

"And how do you propose to do that? You seem to have forgotten, we don't even know where the *Cosmos* is."

The old scientist harrumphed mightily, but I could see that I had scored a point.

"M'sieur Borel's right, Doctor," said Fred, surprisingly coming to my side. "I think I got this thing figured out; the bad Martians want to steal the land of the good Martians who've treated us well so far. What's wrong about giving our friends a hand?"

"It's not that simple, Fred."

"But sometimes it is, Doctor. In my book, those southerners deserve a good lesson. I don't mind giving it to them."

"Let me talk to the King, Doctor," I said, sensing our friend's weakening resolve. "I understand your objections, but none of us want to be stuck on this world forever..."

I turned towards the Great Razaiou and explained that the Doctor's reservations were dictated purely by the fact that, as scientists, we knew nothing about warfare, and thought we might be in the way. I said that of course, we would be happy to lend whatever moral support we could, and would gladly travel alongside them in our ship.

My diplomatic intervention was extremely well-received, and the Great Razaiou was immensely pleased. Orders were given that we were to depart that very evening, and Tiziraou and his men were instructed to finish the work and bring the *Cosmos* to the city.

That night, we drove away from Musiolii, back in our own craft for the first time since our capture.

The Great Razaiou and his war council led the way in an impressive armored vehicle, leading a convoy of troop transports. I was told that five *million* Martians had already been mobilized and sent to the battlefield!

We followed in the *Cosmos*. We had to drive the vehicle ourselves since the Martians' long and fragile tentacled fingers could never have handled the steering. But the King was no fool. We had three extra passengers on board: Tiziraou and our two Macrocephale guides.

Tiziraou was delighted to see our ship run from the inside. He could barely contain his enthusiasm when we hit the great plains to the south of the city. Our traction and speed were more than adequate to keep up with the Martian vehicles, and this new way of travelling filled him with glee.

Loziou and Boulanoi, on the other hand, exhibited no curiosity or interest, and provided very little conversation. Fred quickly nicknamed them "fish face one" and "fish face two" because of their attitude.

It took three days of solid travel before we reached the front. Along the way, we were joined by other troop convoys, but the trip was otherwise eventless.

During that time, the Doctor had made a discreet check and found that his *temporal rotor* and *vector generator* were missing. He grudgingly conceded that I had been right to humor the King and go along with his plan.

I have to say that he did not seem so upset anymore at the notion of watching a Martian war. During the journey, he continued to ingratiate himself with Tiziraou, perhaps in the hopes of finding out what had happened to his missing devices, or to learn more about Martian weapons.

We finally arrived upon an immense plain that was covered with the Northern Martian armies as far as the eye could see. It was a very impressive sight.

On the road, I had had time to ask myself what war on Mars would be like. I dare say that my curiosity was shared by the Doctor and Fred alike...

Could these small, weak men fight with their fragile limbs and tentacled fingers? I did not think so. Instead, I imagined powerful Martian war machines launched at each other at great speed, spewing out deadly rays, clashing in a cacophony of death and destruction... A Wagnerian spectacle of epic proportions...

I was, in fact, rather mistaken, as I shall soon explain.

After our arrival, the Great Razaiou and his council positioned themselves on top of a large observation tower which had been erected behind metal shields in order to safely survey the battlefield.

Soon after, a messenger arrived, mounted on a small floating vehicle that could zoom at great speed along the plain.

"*Ozaia! Ozaia!*" he said, which translated as "Here they come!... here they come!"

The Great Razaiou, firm at his post, issued the final marching orders.

I then observed the Martian troops forming three huge forward lines, each comprised of thousands of soldiers, all marching on foot like mechanical toys. Behind them stood another square formation of perhaps half a million more combatants, ready to be thrown into the fires of battle if the need arose.

The Doctor, Fred and I took our positions on a smaller platform located next to the Great Razaiou's. From that vantage point, we could see the enemy army approaching on the horizon.

They, too, were advancing on foot, like Roman legions or clockwork soldiers.

It seemed almost incomprehensible to me that a race that had produced so many advanced vehicles and machines chose to fight in such a primitive fashion—and yet that was their custom.

As Tiziraou explained, war was a struggle between individuals. The way they saw it, only individuals, not machines, could win. Were the Macrocephales to use their technology to triumph in this conflict, then their enemies would not recognize the victory and surrender accordingly.

But such a war was hardly a bloodless war...

The plain before me was now crisscrossed by zigzagging rays of death. Thousands of red beams and green beams flashed before my eyes without interruption, like a prodigious display of fireworks. Hundreds of bodies twisted and burned everywhere I looked.

The battle had begun, but instead of the din of Earth combat, it was a silent ballet of death, the likes of which I had never seen before...

The Northern Martians used their camera-like boxes to shoot deadly red beams at their enemies, as Roman legionnaires used their pilums to hack at the barbarians.

The Southrons struck back with a similar device that shot green beams.

Both weapons were totally soundless. The Martians, unlike human soldiers, did not scream in rage, anger–or pain. They just mercilessly advanced upon each other, shooting wave after wave of murderous light–and died without even a whimper.

It was an eerily silent battle, one without the cries and clanging of weapons that I had come to expect. The only signs of bloodshed were the slow mowing down of row after row of Martians, like a field of wheat falling before an invisible scythe.

The smell of the half-burned bodies started wafting towards us. It was acrid and stomach-churning, and I had to put my handkerchief to my nose to stop myself from throwing up...

I now could feel the heat of the battle upon my face, literally, as if I had stepped too close to a giant fire...

I then realized that the Southrons were winning the war, and that the front line was moving ever closer towards us.

I could now take a better look at the enemy, who looked entirely like our own Macrocephales. I could not have told them apart, if it had not been for their weapons.

Nothing was more frightening than the sight of each little Martian activating his deadly box, displaying no visible emotions, releasing that merciless lance of death that would burn everything it touched within a hundred meters...

They decimated their enemy carefully, methodically, as we would exterminate an ant colony... It was a frightful sight...

A black cloud of smoke now rose from the killing fields... The once-vast army of the Great Razaiou seemed decimated... Huge swathes of his soldiers had been vaporized by the Southrons...

I noticed a plethora of tiny bursts of light in the distance, and saw that they were caused by the rearguard of the enemy who systematically incinerated the partially burned bodies as they moved methodically across the battlefield.

During all this, one may well be entitled to suppose that the Great Razaiou had become despondent or even yielded to panic...

But no... The King and his council just nodded their heads, now accepting their defeat as a scientific inevitability. Such resignation would have been inconceivable on Earth, where even the most trivial of sporting events is sometimes contested as if life itself depended on its outcome... Here on Mars, war was more like chess, where defeat before an overwhelming force is usually conceded with good grace...

As the front line continued to come dangerously close, the Great Razaiou climbed down from his observation perch and gave the signal for retreat.

Tiziraou explained that we had lost and that, upon our return to Musiolii, the King would contact his counterpart and agree to his demands.

In other words, the war was over. The Southrons had squashed the Northern Macrocephales.

This is when the event that was to determine the course of the next few years of my life and so profoundly affect all our existences happened.

Before, some of the rays shot by the Southrons had hit the metal shields erected by the Northern Macrocephales, and had melted and twisted its metal.

However, no ray had hit the *Cosmos*.

That changed just as we were preparing to reembark to return to the city. Two green rays, one after the other, came whistling by us and struck our ship.

Much to my amazement, they were absorbed like ink disappears inside a blotter!

There was a small flash of pure white light and a sizzling sound, not unlike that of a red hot poker suddenly plunged into a bucket of water, but the coruscating energy of the weapons sank into the outside shell of our craft without a trace.

Even the Doctor was impressed.

"Doctor... Did you see that?" I exclaimed.

The old scientist leaned forward and touched the place where one of the beams had struck. It was obviously unharmed and cold beneath his fingers.

"Hmm... Yes... It is one of the properties of stellite... Otherwise how could it isolate us from the energies that exist outside the continuum... But one is never sure..."

The Doctor was not the only one to be impressed... The Martians were mightily interested by everything that had to do with metals, and I could immediately tell that Tiziraou and the others had taken notice of our craft's seeming invulnerability to their enemies' weapons.

Loziou and Boulanoi, in particular, made excited noises. Loziou left in a hurry and quickly returned with the Great Razaiou and his advisors in tow.

Despite his outward composure, I cannot help but feel that the King had not been pleased by his defeat, and now he was made even more unhappy at being taken away from his vehicle just as he was preparing to return to his palace.

But after he listened to the hurried explanations of the two Macrocephales, I could see that his demeanor lightened up considerably...

He walked up close to the *Cosmos* and touched the spot where the energy bolts had hit the hull.

He then ordered one of his soldiers to fire at the ship, and the same phenomenon occurred. The stellite plainly absorbed the energy of the Martian weapons.

Needless to say, neither the Doctor nor I saw this as a fortunate development. We both anticipated and feared what was to come next...

Indeed, the Great Razaiou then turned towards us, and first thanked us profusely for our immense contribution to his war effort. We had just saved his Kingdom. More importantly, we had saved his people from likely starvation...

The King gave orders that, upon our return to Musiolii, the stellite shell that covered the outside of our craft was to be carefully removed and used to make shielding for his troops.

With that, the war was not lost after all, and victory over the Southrons was certain.

"But, your majesty," the Doctor said, "without the stellite, our ship will no longer be able to traverse the vast distances of space and time that we crossed to come here. We shall be stranded on your planet."

However, it was clear from the onset that our wishes weighed little against the fate of the Macrocephales...

The Great Razaiou assured us that his scientists would make more stellite–it was only a matter of time, he said–and in the meantime, we would be honored as only saviors of the realm could be.

Even though there was little point in arguing against the King, I was preparing to launch myself into another argument, when Fred discretely nudged me to show that our craft was now surrounded by Martians armed with their deadly little boxes.

Of all of us, the Doctor seemed to be the one the most resigned to putting our fate once more in the hands of the Martians, which surprised and even angered me a little.

So it was with a heavy heart that we climbed back into the *Cosmos*. This time, our escort numbered five: Tiziraou, Loziou, Boulanoi plus two armed Martian workers.

There was no doubt in my mind that these had been sent to insure that we would comply with their sovereign's orders and return to the city.

As we drove away on the plains of Mars, I reflected that all our efforts had finally come to an end...

For a while, I had entertained the hope–as crazy as it now seemed–that we would be able to return to our world safe and sound... But now that hope was clearly revealed as futile... I was fated to die on Mars...

But as always, I had underestimated Doctor Omega's craftiness!

We took turns driving the *Cosmos*. While one of us was at the wheel, the other two usually rested in their respective cabins, or conversed with Tiziraou whom, as far as one could read a Martian's expression, was sincerely sorry for the recent turn of events.

The Martian scientist spent a great deal of time promising us that all the resources at his disposal would be brought upon to manufacture more stellite.

The Doctor nodded as if in agreement, but I could see that he was convinced that this was but an illusion, and would never happen. Making stellite was, it seemed, far beyond the reach of Martian technology.

While we were alone in our cabin, the Doctor suddenly leaned towards me with a conspiratorial look.

"During your next shift, Borel, I want you to distract all our guests," he whispered.

"What do you mean?"

"Engage as many as you can in conversation... Show them something of interest on the road... Simulate an accident... I don't know... Use your imagination, young man..."

"But why? Do you have a plan?" I said with renewed excitement.

"Not so loud, you'll attract attention... Yes, I do have a plan... But for that I need to have our companions safely secured, and if you don't mind my saying so, Fred is far more able than you to achieve that result, which is why we need to make our move during your shift..."

"I see," I said, even though I had no idea what the wily scientist really had in mind. "You can count on me, Doctor."

It was clear that Doctor Omega meant to regain control of the *Cosmos*, but what that would achieve without a *temporal rotor*, I had no idea.

By the time it was my turn to take over the wheel, however, I had devised a plan of action.

On the way to the battlefield, I had noticed that we had been instructed to skirt around the zone of the geysers of blue fire that we had encountered before, when we were on our way to the industrial city.

This time, I feigned carelessness and knowingly drove our ship into that perilous landscape, as if by mistake.

As soon as the first balls of fire began to erupt around us, all five Macrocephales became terrified. They waved their tentacled hands in the air, and uttered small shrieks of terror.

"Don't worry," I said in Martian. "I made a navigational error but we've been here before... You don't have anything to fear... I will drive us out... You'll be safe..."

In spite of my words of reassurance, the Martians huddled tighter into their seats, looking through the portholes of our ship with eyes opened wide in fear...

So absorbed by their safety had they become that they failed to notice that Fred had left the bridge and silently returned with a spool of metal wire.

A few seconds later, the deed was done.

Our large friend swung loops of wire over the Martians and easily managed to tie them up. The ones who were armed had no time to use their black boxes.

"What's good for the goose is good for the gander, eh?" said Fred, looking at his work with great satisfaction, remembering how we had been similarly and ignominiously tied on the floor before.

As soon as Fred had acted, I had swerved around and redirected the *Cosmos* westward, away from both the fire zone and the Great Razaiou's Kingdom.

The time had come to regain our freedom.

The Martians seemed more relieved to no longer be facing the threat of the fire geysers than upset by their captivity. They appeared to accept their new status without a struggle, just as the King had accepted his defeat... There was a sense of fatality in their race that was utterly inhuman...

Doctor Omega felt compelled to address our captives and reassure them, especially Tiziraou who had always behaved very decently towards us.

He apologized profusely for being forced to take them prisoner, but explained that as much as we wished, we just could not grant their King's request. The time had come for us to return home. But as soon as we were at a safe distance from both Kingdom and battlefield, they would be released safe and sound.

The Macrocephales drew confidence from that little speech and gave us no trouble. On the contrary, Boulanoi even suggested that we drive to the Pass of Nesrith, a destination which he said would be safe for us, and convenient for them. He gave me directions that would help us circumvent any unsafe conditions along the way.

Only Tiziraou seemed unhappy. I thought that he was genuinely sad to see us leave.

As you shall soon learn, I was grossly mistaken...

"I'm glad to learn that we're going home, Doctor," I said, "but how are you planning to achieve this without your *temporal rotor*?"

"I owe you an apology, Borel," the old scientist replied. "And to you too, Fred."

"An apology? What for?"

"I lied to you by letting you believe that our hosts had taken the *temporal rotor* and *vector generator* away."

"But they did. You said yourself that you saw them take the ship apart after we were captured..."

"Ah, but you see, when I was alone in the *Cosmos*, after you two had gone out to disable the heat ray that was focused on us, the first thing I did was to remove the real *temporal rotor* and *vector generator* and replace them with copies... I hid them in a secret compartment in my cabin–one that could not be found even by taking the ship apart, since it appears to be made of a single piece... Wait here..."

Upon so saying, the Doctor left the bridge.

Fred and I were dumbfounded by this revelation. We became even more astonished when the scientist returned a few minutes later holding what looked indeed like the same complicated devices of metal and glass that I had seen before.

"*Voila!*" said the Doctor triumphantly.

"Wait a minute," I said indignantly. "If you knew you had these machines safely stored away, why, we could have left at any time since we got the *Cosmos* back in Musiolii! You lied to us when you said we couldn't leave, and you didn't want to go to war!"

The Doctor seemed a little guilty and replied sheepishly, "Well, I did mean what I said... We would have left if the King had forced us to take a more active part in the battle... But since you had convinced him to let us be mere observers, Borel, and I was curious to see..."

"I see. Say no more, Doctor! One day, your curiosity will kill us all!"

"You're only a fiddler, young man. What do you know about science and exploration!"

To be called a fiddler, I gathered, was about as bad a thing as the Doctor could think of throwing back at me. But I was so relieved to be able to return to Earth that I could not find it in my heart to remain upset at the old scientist.

After all, everything had turned out for the best, hadn't it?

The Doctor then crawled on the floor under the steering wheel and began working on the reinstallation of the two machines in their proper locations.

From that point on, it took us just under two hours to reach the Pass of Nesrith. Thanks to Boulanoi's directions, we avoided a huge forest of the type we had encountered in the North, which we could otherwise have crossed only at night, and thus saved precious time.

By then, the Doctor had finished the installation of the *temporal rotor* and *vector generator*.

The time had come to honor our word.

We stopped by the side of the road. We were near a rocky canyon, with very little vegetation. It reminded me of some lonely alpine valley. In the distance, I could see the lights of a lonely outpost which Loziou said was either a weather station or an observatory. Our guests could walk there safely.

The Macrocephales, who were not used to the cold, stood shivering like wet dogs on the side of the road and made a rather pitiful sight.

Fred, who was a big-hearted man without malice, gave each of them a blanket, and they were greatly appreciative of his generosity.

"So this is really good-bye?" I asked the Doctor.

"Yes... As soon as we're ready, we'll leave Mars and return to Earth... Unless you'd rather we stayed here some more, young man, hmm?"

That last sarcasm may just have been his way of sniping back at me for my earlier criticisms, but I was so happy at the thought of returning to Earth and seeing my Normandy cottage and my dearest Stradivarius again that I did not even mind.

Suddenly, I was taken by a grim premonition... I have, as you, my readers, have by now realized, an anxious nature, but I am also very intuitive, probably due to my artistic temperament... At that instant, something told me that my hopes were about to be squashed again... That something bad was about to happen... There are thoughts that come unwanted inside our heads in a preternatural fashion, as if an unknown force takes pleasure in opening the shutters of our minds to reveal brief glimpses of the future when it knows it can most hurt us...

That moment happened to me when Tiziraou, who had barely said a word since his capture, stepped towards us.

"Do not go," he said. "The metallic composition of your stellite (he used our word for he had no Martian equivalent) has been changed by the *Lozi* (the death rays). Your craft is not safe."

I could see the Doctor pale. He began to ask the Martian some questions, and while I understood nothing of the scientific conversation that ensued, I knew deep inside myself that Tiziraou had to be right.

The Doctor climbed aboard the craft and came out holding a tool that buzzed as he slowly passed it over the portions of the ship which had been struck by the energy beams.

While outwardly there had been no visible impact, my musician's ear told me that the slight variations in the buzzing were indicative of a transformation in our hull.

The Doctor finally turned towards us, looking dejected, his head lowered, grimmer than I had ever seen him before.

"Tiziraou is correct," he said in a grave voice. "The stellite has become temporally porous. My synthesis was less than perfect, for if it had been, it would not have reacted so to the energy beams... I'm sorry, my friends... Our last hope of returning to Earth is no more..."

Chapter Eleven
Stranded!

It took Doctor Omega several more hours to run additional tests on the composition of the stellite hull that covered the exterior surface of the *Cosmos*, and without which we had no hope of surviving the rigors of our journey outside the space-time continuum. But the results remained the same.

Somehow, the Martian energy beams had altered the properties of that strange metal, and our ship was no longer safe.

In fact, by warning us, Tiziraou had saved us from a horrible death.

For the first time since our initial encounter, I began to feel that the Doctor was truly defeated, and that possibility frightened me even more than the prospect of ending my life on this ghastly planet.

"Our only option is to return to the Macrocephales' city," he said glumly to Fred and me. "By delivering our craft to them, the Razaiou can still manufacture energy-absorbing shields for his army and win his war against the Southrons."

"Surrender to these gnomes?" said Fred, dumb-founded. "But the little monsters are going to kill us..."

"No. The Razaiou will forgive our flight, I think, especially since Tiziraou has given me his assurances that he will not reveal our plight, and instead tell his King that we had misunderstood his intentions."

"So we're condemned to spend the rest of our lives here?" I asked dejectedly.

"Unless we're rescued..." began the Doctor.

"Then we might as well get used to the fact that we'll die on this planet."

"You're a very depressing fellow, Borel. You know nothing about the vast realm of possibilities that still exist out there..."

"I know you think I'm only a 'fiddler,' as you called me, Doctor, and yes, I'm not a scientist like you, and I don't know what's out there, but who else but an artist like me would have chosen to accompany you on such a crazy expedition? If you don't mind my saying so, I think any man more reasonable than I would have laughed at you, or thought twice about journeying to another world. So please, give me a little credit for my enthusiasm if not for my lack of optimism..."

The Doctor harrumphed but said nothing.

Our return journey was filled with gloom... Our faces were drawn, and the joyful confidence of the previous day had been replaced by an almost palpable sense of disappointment. Only our Martian escorts did not hide their joy at the thought of soon being reunited with their brethren, and helping their people win the war.

As we approached the industrial city, we noticed that the Southron armies had progressed far into the Macrocephales' territory. We encountered signs of other battles, obviously last-ditch efforts by our allies to stem the tide of their impending defeat.

We came across what must have been metal fortresses, turned now into charred and twisted metal wrecks. Billows of pungent, black smoke hung morbidly in the air like shrouds, marking the battlefields where countless Martian troops had undoubtedly lost their lives.

We finally reached the factory and as soon as we stepped out of the *Cosmos*, Tiziraou began issuing orders to his crew of diminutive workers.

In the space of a few minutes, our craft had become a beehive of frantic activity, with some Martians busily removing the outer layers of stellite, while others carried the plates to far sections of the plant where they would be reshaped into hair-thin platings for the shields that had been designed.

With Tiziraou hard at work on creating the new equipment, we understood that our presence at the factory was no longer necessary. The Doctor had once again removed his *temporal rotor* and *vector generator* which he now carried in a small black bag.

Loziou and Boulanoi found an electric car and offered to take us back to our previous quarters in Musio-lii.

We therefore returned to the Martian capital, and my heart sank when, at long last, I saw the metal spires that only a day before I had so foolishly thought to leave behind; I could not prevent my fist from clenching out of pure frustration.

As to Fred, I saw his head bowed in defeat, and I thought I might even have seen his eyes glisten as if he was trying to repress tears.

The streets and squares of the city were thick with Martians of all classes. Our return must have been reported somehow, for there were crowds eager to see us... However, I could not tell if they were happy at the thought of us having brought back the means to destroy their enemies, or angry at our earlier desertion...

We were soon left to our own devices in our apartments, while our Martian escort no doubt rushed to give the news to the Great Razaiou.

We thus spent several days alone, with no contact with any Martians, other than the *noussaï* who brought us our nutrition pills every day.

At night, on the balconies, we could see the smoke of battles far on the horizon, and occasionally we spied the lights of energy weapon discharges, like far-away thunderbolts, but we had no idea how the war was going.

I began to worry that our returning with the stellite might have come too late to save the Macrocephales. What if they lost and we became prisoners of the Southrons instead? Surely, we had cast our lot with the Great Razaiou, and had little mercy to expect from the other side...

Fred, on the other hand, believed that he was strong enough to secure our escape if the city fell into enemy hands. To that effect, the big man trained relentlessly in the gardens, and had regained his prodigious physical shape.

Doctor Omega, in the meantime, had chosen to absorb himself in scientific work, the nature of which I could not fathom. If you recall, our friend had had the Martians build him a work bench in his room, and throughout our stay had collected various bits of machinery.

He was now busily at work, cannibalizing parts from his *temporal rotor* and soldering them together into a contraption that looked like one of De Dion-Bouton's modern engines, but less elegant.

When I asked him what he was doing, he merely rebuffed me with his usual gruffness, and advised me to be patient, or told me that he was not yet ready to reveal what he was working on, for fear of disappointing us.

Finally, on the seventh night, the Doctor called Fred and me to his room, his fine brow still softly glistening from the sweat of the soldering iron.

"Tonight, my friends," he announced. "Yes, tonight we shall attempt a great experiment... I will need your help to carry this machine to the terrace... Then, when Earth is high in the sky, I shall send our first message..."

Seeing our incredulous expressions, he explained:

"Yes... I have managed to build a... a telegraph, if you will... One that uses waves that travel through the space-time continuum like light through the emptiness of space... With this machine, there is nothing that prevents me from reaching Earth... There is the power source... The electrodes... The transduction coils... The receivers... I only need to raise the directional antenna to send a signal... My one fear is that I may not have enough power... But I can always steal more power cells, so even that should not be an issue..."

"You mean to send an S.O.S... But will there be anyone to receive it, Doctor?"

The old scientist looked craftily at me.

"We will soon find out, won't we, young man?" he said, which naturally explained nothing, but restored my faith in the abilities of this amazing man to extricate us from even the most desperate of situations.

However, my heart sank again when suddenly, Loziou and Boulanoi showed up, walked gravely towards us and said that the Great Razaiou wished to see us.

We followed them to the throne room... While walking, I tried to inquire about the fate of the war, but they stayed silent and did not answer any of my questions.

We were ushered into the same sumptuous throne room that we had admired so much only a few weeks before.

At first glance, I suspected that the Great Razaiou was angry. Little dark green veins pulsated on his massive forehead, and the slit that was his mouth was more circonflexed and quivered in a fashion that I found ill-omened; his thin tentacled fingers gripped his crystal scepter nervously, and his tiny, twiggy legs shook with uncontrollable spasms.

The Doctor walked up to the throne and performed the usual salutations.

"Great King... We salute you..."

"Why did you three *Babazeio* leave my Kingdom without my express permission," grumbled the Razaiou, "taking with you five of my subjects, and the absorbing metal that covers your *mayoclei*?"

I tried to present our case, but the King who, in the past, had welcomed my intervention, rebuffed me.

"Keep quiet, wily *Babazeio*, and let the learned *gayado* (he meant the Doctor) answer."

I stepped back a few paces and saluted confusedly.

225

The Doctor understood that the situation was serious, and once again handled himself with his usual self-composed assurance. With well-chosen and measured words, he explained to the King that, far from trying to desert him, we had sought to hurry back to the industrial city to speed up the manufacture of the protective shields—as Tiziraou himself would verify. We had run afoul of the geysers of blue fire, and had had to secure his men who were panicking and threatening our efforts.

I could see that the Great Razaiou was becoming increasingly relaxed as he listened attentively to the Doctor's presentation of our case.

The old scientist knew how to make a point and ended his speech with the proclamation that the best proof of our innocence, nay, our desire to help our hosts, was our speedy return to the factory when it would have been easy for us to flee to other destinations, or even join forces with the Southrons, if such had been our intentions.

By then, the King was swinging his head slowly back and forth, like a serpent, which I had learned to recognize as the Martian equivalent of a nod.

The Doctor's eloquence, as effective as any I had ever heard from a Master of the Bar at the *Palais de Justice*, had carried the day.

To drive his point even further, the Doctor went as far as to complain loudly that we had been seeking news of the war since we had returned, but had been kept purposefully in the dark... We, who had strived to deliver their ultimate weapon to the Macrocephales, were not told if our stellite had indeed contributed to their victory. We had watched the signs of battle far away with heavy hearts, not knowing if our help had been in time.

The Razaiou let out a long, deep sigh which was his way of expressing approval and regret simultaneously. He ordered the attendants, who had been whispering among themselves, to grow quiet.

"Learned *garagoulô*," he began, reverting to the term meaning honored guest, "you speak the truth... The Great Razaiou owes you and your two companions the gratitude of the Kingdom... You came from the Blue Star to deliver us from the Southron menace... Thanks to your absorbing metal, my armies overcame the Southrons and drove them back to their cities the day before yesterday..."

Then, speaking to his servants, he ordered: "Display the great dome so that our *garagoulô* friends can see the extent of our victory!"

Suddenly, the curved ceiling lit up and became a convex map of Mars' northern hemisphere, like the inside of a planetarium.

By pointing with his scepter and moving it like a baton, the Razaiou was able to illuminate certain features on the map, or drag it around.

We saw the capital where we were, surrounded by the industrial cities and the vast expanse of agricultural lands. The King pointed out the battlefield where we had witnessed the obliteration of his first army...

Then, moving the map to the south, he showed us his counter-attack, and how his forces had gained control of an increasingly larger portion of the Southrons' territories.

We feigned interest, even enthusiasm, at the tale of the Macrocephales' triumph.

Finally, having shared his latest accomplishments with us, the Great Razaiou turned off the ceiling display and turned towards us again.

"This, I owe to you, *garagoulô*, and from this day onward you will be my honored guests and will work to perfect other inventions from your planet that will serve the glory of my people. I will have a special city built for your discoveries, and many of our *noussaï* will be placed at your disposal...I no longer want my precious guests to risk their lives outside... You will stay in the capital where every one of your wishes will be fulfilled by our *giiloï*... Anything you ask for will be provided to you... I have spoken..."

I thought to myself that either the King had not, after all, entirely believed the Doctor's story, or our value to him had become so great that, in either case, we had become prisoners in a gilded cage...

As I pondered over this, the Razaiou's throne floated backwards on its invisible rails and disappeared behind a wall of light.

Loziou and Boulanoi escorted us back to our quarters, displaying even greater signs of respect... For until the new factory was built, this had become our permanent residence...

All hope for a new escape in the *Cosmos* was now useless... We were, and would remain, prisoners of the Macrocephales, unless the Doctor's space-time telegraph could somehow summon help.

The old scientist, unlike Fred and I, did not appear particularly upset by this new turn of events. His face was calm and his eyes betrayed no emotion. It was as if nothing out of the ordinary had happened.

"What do you think, Doctor?" I could not help asking. "Do you believe that your..."

"Hush, young man! Our hosts are not stupid. These two are listening to us, obviously. No one must suspect what we're planning... No one, you hear me! Otherwise the Razaiou will take steps to close even that last avenue of escape..."

After eating our ration of nutrition pills that evening, Fred and I gathered in the Doctor's room. Since the Razaiou had ordered that we work on creating more Terran weapons, no one had disturbed the old scientist's equipment.

Fred and I carried the machine to the terrace, and the Doctor began a series of long adjustments of the antenna, pointing it towards the Blue Star shining in the Martian firmament that we knew was Earth.

I had never seen him so nervous as he kept tinkering with his machine, presumably sending signals into the aether.

We thus spent the whole night with his telegraph without any visible result... Every hour, the Doctor sent more transmissions towards Earth, or more accurately into space... Then, after each transmission, he became motionless, his face glued to the receiver, fixed in intense concentration...

Fred and I eventually fell asleep... When daybreak came, we found the old scientist sitting before his machine, just as we had left him. His features were drawn and paler than usual, but he looked as determined as ever...

I approached him and put my hand on his shoulder.
"Anything?"
"Not yet," he replied.
"You really think that someone is listening? I don't know if..." I began, not managing to hide my incredulity.
The Doctor interrupted me with one of his irritated looks.

"There are many things that you don't know, Borel, and frankly I have neither the inclination nor the patience of explaining them to you."

He then turned around and, without another glance, returned to his watch.

I realized that I had once again angered him by openly expressing my doubts. It was an act of petty revenge, motivated by the fact that I blamed him, unfairly, for my predicament... Yet I could not help myself, even though I knew all too well that one should never underestimate him...

For the next eight nights, Doctor Omega directed his mysterious transmissions towards the place in space and time where Earth was, and yet received only total silence in return, not even the slightest bit of static...

During that time, our moods alternated between despair and irrational optimism... There were times when I abandoned all hope, dismissed the notion of interplanetary communication, and thought that the Doctor's signals were simply fated to become lost in the infinity of space and time... I felt pity towards the old scientist as I was convinced of the utter futility of his efforts...

Yet, at other times, I could not help but admire his perseverance... His unshakable faith in the very science that seemed to betray him... His deep conviction that he would ultimately be vindicated...

He never lost faith, not for a single instant; every night, he spent time rotating his dials, fine-tuning his signal, boosting his transmission with more power cells kindly provided by the unsuspecting Martians...

He had built a clever automated system that now broadcast our S.O.S. all day on rotating frequencies, and a buzzing system that would alert us in the event of a response...

"Don't lose faith, Borel... You'll see... Sooner or later, it will ring...I'm sure of it... It can't be otherwise."

I refrained from making any more negative remarks, and usually redirected the conversation towards one or the other of his other current projects.

Yet, I could see that the old scientist was becoming increasingly depressed, he, too, abandoning hope and losing himself in idle scientific chatter during his long daily sessions with the friendly Tiziraou, with whom he had developed quite a mutual rapport.

I had to find a way to redirect his prodigious mind and focus his energies on solving our predicament. So I decided against all hope to persuade him to find a way to build a new *Cosmos*.

One morning, after our breakfast, in truth the absorption of a single nutrition, pill, we took a walk in the gardens below, shadowed by our Martian helpers.

After telling the Doctor that I was still placing great hopes in his telegraph (which, candidly, was a barefaced lie), I asked him what were the chances of him building a new ship.

I could see him think long and deeply before he answered: "It's far more difficult than you suspect... The craft itself is easy to assemble... Tiziraou has all the designs, and we've become so friendly that I think he has become sympathetic to our plight... But synthesizing the stellite without the equipment I left behind on Earth would be virtually impossible... It would be like asking one of your primitive tribes to manufacture a finely tuned Swiss watch, Borel..."

"But not entirely impossible, Doctor... With the right help... And with you in charge of it, of course..." For I knew that appealing to his scientific vanity would spur him into action.

"Perhaps you're right... These Martians are prodigious engineers... I would have to create the tools that in turn would manufacture the other tools required for the task... But Tiziraou would help... And the Razaiou would support my research... But even if I could overcome all the obstacles, it still would take years..."

"Time is something we have plenty of at the moment, Doctor."

The old scientist smiled, and this was the first smile I had seen on his face in days, so I felt heartened at the success of my plan.

"I'm grateful to you, young man," he said, shaking my hand with emotion. "You were right to force me to think again in that direction... I'm afraid I've grown too distracted lately... Now you've given me new purpose... I'll start working on it this very day!"

But luck, as they say, is a capricious mistress, and we would never, in fact, discover if the Doctor would have been capable of building a new craft, for that same night I received the surprise of my life.

In the midst of darkness, I was suddenly roughly awakened by the Doctor... His voice sounded unusually excited and enthusiastic.

"Wake up, Borel! Wake up! She's heard me! Yes, she's heard me! And she's answered!"

"Who? Who's heard you? What are you talking about?"

"Susanne... Susanne's received my message!"

I thought the Doctor had completely lost his mind. But he pulled me out of bed and dragged me towards his telegraph, which was indeed buzzing with a series of low clicks and pings that I took to be a signal like Morse code...

Indeed, my trained ear detected a repetition in the pattern of the sounds that emanated from the machine.

The Doctor had transcribed these sounds on a Martian tablet but it looked just like a series of squiggles to me.

"What does that say?" I asked.

"It's written in the language of my people... It says: *Message received. Send coordinates. Susanne.*"

"Who is Susanne?"

"My granddaughter whom I left studying in Paris at the *Pension Clavel*... She must have returned to my laboratory in Normandy... I have another machine there, similar to this one, which is always plugged in... She obviously found my messages..."

"Are you certain?"

"How can you even question it? Have you gone mad, Borel? Look at the evidence of your own eyes... These are the receivers... The dials... The antenna... The signal definitely comes from Earth... From our own space and time... Ah! You thought that my telegraph was useless... No, don't deny it, I knew perfectly well what you were thinking... But I was right! It was only a matter of time and perseverance... Our captivity nears its end, my friends!"

In the meantime, Fred had walked into the room and had heard the end of the Doctor's speech.

Upon registering the impact of the scientist's last words, he began shaking his hand like a water pump; then, grabbing me with his other hand, he began dragging us in a mad *farandole* dance across the room.

I gave in to the general elation, rejoicing that we had at last succeeded in communicating with Earth...

Our S.O.S. had finally been heard!

Indeed, I had thought the Doctor deluded... fooling himself about his chances of ever reaching across the aether to our homeworld... And once again, I had grossly underestimated the power of his mind.

I should have known that Doctor Omega was a pure genius, on the same level as a Newton, a Mariotte, a Ruhmkorff, an Edison or a Marconi... He had synthesized the fabulous stellite that had taken us on this most extraordinary of journeys... He had designed the *Cosmos*, aboard which we had crossed the vast gulfs of time and space...

I was ashamed to have again questioned his brilliance, and the only thing I can say in my defense is that it has always been in my sensitive nature to question and worry...

But, in typical fashion, after these moments of great joy, we experienced another series of setbacks.

For an entire Martian month thereafter, Doctor Omega sent nearly five hundred messages to his granddaughter, but received no replies. Not a single message.

At that point, I again almost lost confidence in my old friend, and began to ask myself if he had not made up that first message from his granddaughter, perhaps merely to give us hope, or to prove himself right... I found it difficult to accept that we could not talk to Mademoiselle Susanne as if she were at the other end of a telephone line...

The Doctor patiently explained to me that, while it was relatively easy for his equipment to broadcast to the other machine once he had locked in its signal, it was very difficult for Susanne to respond in kind, since our transmission was very faint, travelling as I had presumed over vast distances of space and time through the continuum.

Then I wondered if maybe the Doctor had not made some kind of error in the assembling of his telegraph... Was his machine inadequate for the task?

Fortunately, late one afternoon, the buzzer finally vibrated again and the three of us sat entranced before the equipment while the Doctor carefully transcribed the series of clicks and pings that issued from the receivers.

I again expected a burst of exuberance like the one that had followed the reception of the first message from Susanne, and with my heart uplifted, prepared to share in the collective joy; instead, much to my consternation, the Doctor remained frozen on the spot like a statue. He seemed not elated but frustrated...

"What's wrong?" I asked, my heart squeezed in an icy grip of fear.

The old scientist stayed silent... His eyes were fixed upon the message he had just transcribed in his mysterious cursive script, seemingly hypnotized by its contents.

Then, turning towards us, he explained:

"I might as well be candid with you, Borel... I had thought Susanne might come to our rescue... As Fred knows... And as I told you before we left Earth, my goal in building the *Cosmos* was to create my own craft... One whose stellite would not carry the mark of my people... But desperate situations require desperate measures, and if called to do so, my granddaughter could have used my other ship to travel to Mars... However, she's just informed me that its secondary *temporal rotor* is hopelessly damaged... And, er, you see, I removed the primary rotor to install it in the *Cosmos*... And without a *temporal rotor*..."

"You mean, she can't come after all?" I would almost have cried in despair and frustration.

"She cannot, but *others* can..." said the Doctor softly.

"Others?"

"There's another scientist who has the same... ship... as I... His name is Professor Helvetius... I also call him the Clockmaker, because he spent a great deal of time in Switzerland, although last I heard he was living in England..."

"Is he a friend of yours?"

The Doctor smiled a rather wan smile.

"My people don't have friends, Borel. We rarely reach that degree of closeness with each other... We mostly keep to ourselves..."

I understood, or at least I think I did... Of course, he could not have made many friends among other scientists who would be envious of his genius, fools that would ridicule his discoveries, and even those who would feel threatened by his brilliance, might try to exploit it, like the Great Razaiou had done, or worse, destroy it. No, friendship must indeed have come hard to one such as he...

"As they say, victory finds a hundred fathers but defeat is an orphan..." he added wistfully.

"I think Ovid said something of the kind," I replied.

The old scientist smiled and took both my hands in his.

"Don't pay attention to my maudlin mood, young man... I know I've got two good friends and companions in you and Fred here... Thanks to both of you, I've never felt more confident than in this instant."

"So you think that this Professor Helvetius will help us?"

"Yes, I think so... If my granddaughter can find him, I think he will... She is a very persuasive young lady... "

The Doctor rubbed his hands in glee and added:

"Now, we just have to wait... Let's be patient... We shall maintain this channel of communication open day and night, and it will soon lead Susanne and my colleague to us, almost as surely as a lighthouse beacon guides ships in the night. Trust me, we'll soon be seeing Earth again..."

That night, I fell asleep feeling almost totally reassured... And I had wonderful dreams...

I dreamed that we were back on Earth... A huge crowd was welcoming us, cheering and clapping... A big, important looking man, dressed in formal clothes–probably a minister–was giving the Doctor, Fred and I huge decorations, crosses of diamond with red ribbons that flapped in the wind like flags of victory...

But I was torn from this delicious dream by loud yelling and the sound of trampling feet...

I jumped from my bed and rushed into the corridor.

The first thing I saw was Doctor Omega standing in front of his room, his face livid with anger, his normally slick white hair looking somewhat disheveled, and his clothes in disarray.

I peeked into his room and saw what had provoked his anger: the space-time telegraph was now lying smashed and in pieces on the floor. The coils, the antenna, the receivers, all were now a mass of shapeless, twisted bits, not even crumbs... The disaster was total... irreparable...

Those who had wrecked the prodigious machine had done it so thoroughly that it was totally impossible to reuse any of the debris... The work bench itself had

237

been removed, probably because it could not be smashed... And the improvised pole that we had set up to support the antenna had also been taken.

Loziou and Boulanoi stood there with three *noussaï* behind them, and there was no doubt that those hideous gnomes were the authors of this sabotage...

In fact, I could tell that they looked embarrassed by their actions... Instead of standing straight in the center of the room as they normally did, they were hunched and had slunk into a corner.

"They've destroyed your machine!" shouted Fred, brandishing his fist angrily at the Martians. "Miserable little cowards! Disgusting gnomes! Monsters!"

The big man was going to attack the Martians but the Doctor and I pulled him back, because we had noticed that the three *noussaï* were armed with their deadly little boxes. To strike at them now would have been risking our lives, for even if we had succeeded in overpowering the ones in our room, the Great Razaiou would never have forgiven us for one more transgression...

We finally managed to calm Fred down, and his rage abated somewhat, the big man chose to leave the room, not trusting himself to stay in the company of the Martians.

Loziou stepped forward and delivered the message we expected to hear:

"*Barônioniz Babazeio irvettir maiano* Razaiou *sûliez oïodoûm nhátonoi orónos.*"

Which meant: "It displeases the Great Razaiou to see the Earthmen send beams into space."

Then, they left, or rather scurried away from the room.

I asked the Doctor if he thought there was any possibility that he might secretly reassemble his telegraph. He replied by shaking his head negatively.

"No, young man... Not a hope."

"But without its signal, how will your colleague find us? Are we lost forever?"

"Who knows?" said Doctor Omega, looking at the starry Martian night sky in which the light of the Blue Star which we knew was Earth was beginning to fade as dawn approached.

Chapter Twelve
The Rescue

In the days following the foiling of our escape plan and the destruction of our space-time telegraph by the Martians, we were again isolated ... Even Tiziraou's regular visits stopped... We were left to ponder our fate...

I had now abandoned all hopes of rescue, and as a result, I was continually in a foul mood... Fred, too, had lost his normally sunny disposition... And Doctor Omega, subject to the constant company of what one must admit were two very unhappy companions, also became withdrawn and surly...

Days went by during which we barely exchanged even a few words... I was trying to become used to the fact that I would be spending the rest of my days on Mars, and that detestable notion was not only affecting my mood, as I said, but my health as well! I was in danger of becoming a hypochondriac as I imagined myself suffering from a variety of ailments, each worse than the other...

Then, just as I was reaching the end of my rope, several weeks later, things suddenly took a turn for the better, and from the most unexpected of quarters. But I must not rush ahead of myself and tell you the story of how our escape really happened.

That night, we could not sleep, no matter how hard we tried. The Doctor was idly whiling away time looking at the night skies and the starry constellations as they were billions of years in the past... He had just wished aloud that he had a telescope...

"Well, we don't have one," I responded tetchily. "In fact, as you must have noticed, we don't have much of anything anymore."

The Doctor ignored me with his usual condescension, and I was about to launch myself into another verbal attack, when suddenly he pointed to the gardens below.

"Look, Borel," he exclaimed. "Isn't that Tiziraou?"

"By Jove! I believe it is." Then, after a pause, I continued: "That's very unusual. I don't think he's ever come to visit us in the middle of the night before. I wonder what he wants."

"Perhaps the Razaiou has lifted his orders?" said Fred, who had joined us.

"No, I don't think so," said the Doctor. "If that was the case, he wouldn't be acting so... furtively... Doesn't he look furtive to you, Borel?"

"I think you're right, Doctor... This is very strange indeed..."

"Well, we'll soon know what is going on."

A few minute later, the Macrocephale entered our quarters. He was carrying a small rectangular box, a little smaller than a toolbox, under his arm.

"Tiziraou... My dear colleague... What brings you here so late?" asked the Doctor.

"My Earth friends... I wanted to come and visit you before, but the Great Razaiou has been inflexible... He has ordered that no one is to see you or bring you any *nohaz* (a word which meant machinery or tools)... He is now afraid of your cunning... He fears that you will devise another way to escape..."

"So you are risking his wrath by coming here?" I said.

"Only if I am caught," he replied, and I swore that if he had been an Earthman, he would have winked at us. "But no one knows that I am here. I took great precautions because I wanted to deliver this to you..."

And so saying he placed the metal box over a low table, and pressing an invisible switch on its side, caused its top to shrink away into its four sides.

Inside was a small device that bore a striking resemblance to the bigger and more cumbersome machine that the Doctor had built. Our old friend identified it right away.

"A space-time telegraph! But... How is it possible?..."

Tiziraou looked extremely pleased with himself.

"I was not fooled by what you were doing, and I carefully took notes and *doloû* (pictures, like photographs on metal)... It took me a long time because I am not as great a theorist as you, learned *garagoulô*, but I managed to reconstruct your device..."

243

"Tiziraou... This is splendid... Wonderful... I don't know what to say," I said, not finding the right words to express my astonishment and gratitude.

The Doctor was examining the device closely.

"Amazing... Just amazing... Such miniaturization... This is a work of art, Tiziraou..."

"Thank you. Your praise means much to me."

"Did you tune it to the correct frequency?"

"I think so, but the device has mostly been silent... Except for tonight where it began to communicate again... Which is why I have hurried to bring it to you... I recorded the signals it sent... Let me play them back to you..."

The Macrocephale pressed the receiver with his long finger, and we heard the usual pattern of clicks and pings. Never had any sounds caused so much joy in a room!

The Doctor's eyes stopped looking like dull metal and again began to sparkle. His entire body straightened and became charged with energy, as if quicksilver was suddenly flowing in his veins.

Fred, unable to embrace the little Martian at the risk of crushing him, instead trapped me in a bear hug, almost suffocating me, muttering in a voice almost paralyzed by emotion:

"This time, we're saved... They're coming for us, M'sieur Borel..."

As to me, after a few minutes of incredulity, I felt an incredible joy fill my entire body. I hugged Fred back and both of us began a little dance across the room.

"What does it say, Doctor?" I finally asked.

The old scientist, who had just shushed me with his hand to better hear the last notes, then explained: "This is a message from Professor Helvetius. In about six hours local time, his ship will land on Mars. He wants us to continue broadcasting our signal so that he can locate us with precision."

"Six hours? But it'll be daylight," I said. "He'll be spotted. The Razaiou will order his troops to fire at him, to destroy him!"

"Hmm... You're right, Borel... But I think there's a way to avoid any incidents... We must make a rendez-vous outside the city..."

"That sounds like a fine plan, Doctor, but how can we do that?"

Suddenly, Tiziraou raised his piping voice.

"I anticipated this and secreted a *plooplô* (electric car) outside... I can take you to the Pass of Nesrith... Your friend will be led there by the signals emanating from this machine. You can meet him there in safety... But I want to come with you..."

"You mean, to the Pass of Nesrith?" asked the Doctor, even though we had already exchanged quick glances and suspected what Tiziraou's answer was going to be.

"No. To Earth. I want to see your world. Discover new things, like what you sought to do when you decided to visit my world. I want to be an explorer too. There is nothing more for me to learn on this world..."

Then the little Martian placed his delicate fingers on the Doctor's sleeve.

"You and I have discussed the future of my race, o wise *garagoulô*... I know that you believe that we have reached the end of our evolution... That we shall, in time be replaced by a younger race...Perhaps the *Setissi*, whom you call the Warriors from under the Sea of Ice... You have told me that in your era, our world is a dead planet... My world used to be all that there was and ever

245

would be for me... But now, thanks to you, I know that it is no more than a speck of metal in this great city, ever changing, always different... I am no longer satisfied to stay here... I want to see Earth, and more..."

"Well, er..."

"Come on, Doctor!" I said. "This is great news. Think of the public applause and the scientific acclaim on Earth if we bring back a real live Martian!"

It was as if I had punched the Doctor in the face. He turned towards me, and I had never seen him so grim, even when we had been trapped in the worst of situations.

"I fear I haven't any interest in any public applause, and I don't seek to impress any scientists, young man. If we take Tiziraou with us, it won't be to turn him into one of your zoo specimens, or make him perform like those Native Americans that your explorers once paraded at the court of your Sun King... No, I shall not condone such behavior! Never! Our friend here will be treated with respect, just as another of our companions... I must have your word that we shall protect the secret of his origins when we're back on Earth... Do I have your word, Mister Borel?"

I felt ashamed to have momentarily succumbed to the feelings of vanity that had been made vivid in such a ludicrous fashion in my earlier dream.

"You're right, Doctor," I apologized. "I'm sorry. I don't know where my head was... Of course, you have my word..." Then, I turned to Tiziraou and gave the salute that Martians use when expressing veneration towards a retired elder. "You can trust me, esteemed *Pohozao*... On Earth, your secret shall be safe with us."

Fred, as always, drove the point home with his usual common sense and country wisdom.

"I didn't like it when they put us in a cage here, and I'm not going do the same to the little fella back home."

Having agreed on a course of action, we grabbed whatever few belongings we still had left, including our precious notes and samples, and wearing only the clothes on our back, we followed Tiziraou out.

We crossed the gardens without encountering any obstacles nor meeting any guards. Tiziraou led us to a hidden door inside the very metal of the walls, the existence of which we had never before suspected.

The Macrocephale, however, knew how to open it, and upon his command, an opening formed in the metal. Its size was designed for Martians, not humans, so all three of us, especially Fred, had to crouch to go through it... But since this was literally the way to freedom, none of us dared complain.

As Tiziraou had told us, a small electric car was waiting for us on the other side of the wall.

We all got into it, and the little Martian engineer grabbed the controls, handing the metal box with the still-transmitting space-telegraph to the Doctor.

"We shall reach the Pass of Nesrith in five hours," said the Macrocephale. "An hour before your friend is scheduled to arrive..."

"Let's go, my friends," said the Doctor. "This is truly our last chance for freedom. We must reach the Pass before dawn, no matter what may stand in our way."

A few minutes later, the car was zooming at high speed on the city's metal highways. Tiziraou knew all the backroads and either through his skill or pure luck, we were able to leave the city unnoticed.

We all let out a sigh of relief, because none of us would have wished to be delayed by a confrontation with the Martians, one that could easily have turned deadly.

Once we reached the open countryside, we no longer had any obstacles to fear, and we gained speed rapidly... It took only four and a half hours to reach the lonely rocky valley that we had already visited on our previous, unfortunate attempt to leave Mars.

The night was almost over, but the Martian night is never totally obscure, as I have remarked before, and I could discern the contours of the cliffs and, in the distance, a shiny surface which, I was told, was the waters of Syrtis Major, also called the Hourglass Sea.

My heart began beating even more wildly as dawn slowly arrived and with it, the fateful hour when our rescuers would arrive.

At last, the new day rose... The sky was still milky and the light dim... The landscape around us looked as if we were staring at it through a fogged-up window... The Doctor was pacing back and forth, occasionally checking the space-time telegraph to make sure that its beacon was still transmitting.

Then, as the small, pale orb that was the sun rose higher in the sky, the light became sharper and the morning fog began slowly to dissipate.

Suddenly, I heard a humming noise, like that of a bassoon or a fog horn; my mind conjured up the image of a clumsy violinist trying desperately to rip a melody out of his instrument. It reminded me of the groaning sounds that I had first heard in the Doctor's laboratory when he was synthesizing his stellite...

The bizarre noise came from behind a rocky crag. The Doctor, who did not seem especially surprised, began to trot towards it. Naturally, we followed him.

As we turned the corner, both Fred and I uttered small screams of surprise that echoed amongst the cliffs and to the sea beyond.

Before us stood a huge, metallic grey shape that seemed to stare at us from two big, round, yellow eyes... That thing was not a monster but an artificial construct... It was the *Cosmos*, or rather not our *Cosmos*, but an ever bigger ship, very much like it... It was the rescue ship, the coming of which we had so ardently prayed for so many weeks... The cosmic lifeboat that we thought would never appear... Now, it was standing motionless on the Martian soil, before our very eyes, ready to take us home!

Later, I theorized that it must have landed under the cover of the morning fog, for I had not seen it come down from the sky, but at that moment, that detail mattered little to me.

The ship's oval door opened, revealing an older man and a young girl.

The girl was perhaps twelve or fourteen years of age... She had short black hair and a vivacious face, with an endearingly impish smile... She wore a schoolgirl uniform and she ran towards Doctor Omega shouting: "Grandfather!"

They fell into each other's arms. It was apparent that these two loved each other very much. For a couple of minutes, it was as if no one else existed on the surface of Mars, so happy were they to have found each other again.

Doctor Omega introduced her to me as Susanne, his granddaughter. Smiling, she did a little curtsy to me, and gave Fred a big kiss on his cheek, then went to stand next to her grandfather.

Meanwhile, the older man walked towards the Doctor, his face smiling and his arms extended in welcome. The two scientists shook hands slowly. A deep, powerful feeling of wisdom and mutual respect emanated from them.

Even today, I can't recall that scene without a shiver of tremendous happiness. This is how I met the remarkable Professor Helvetius.

He was an older man who, in many respects, seemed to be cut from the same cloth as Doctor Omega. He was smaller and looked older, although his eyes, which peered through a pair of gold-rimmed spectacles, shone with prodigious intelligence. He wore a mop of unruly white hair, and was dressed in a comfortable tweedy suit of the type often worn by British academics.

Professor Helvetius, like the Doctor, seemed to be incorrigibly curious. Instead of departing right away, he insisted on taking a look at our surroundings, and expressed a great interest in meeting Tiziraou. The Doctor seemed all too oblivious of our predicament, and the three of them discussed nature and philosophy as if they had been walking serenely in the *Jardins des Plantes* in Paris, arguing about the discovery of a new species of dinosaurs...

Fred and I had to remind them somewhat forcefully that the Great Razaiou had probably already discovered our escape, and undoubtedly would be sending his forces after us, so it was in all our best interests to leave as soon as possible.

Common sense prevailed and we all climbed aboard Helvetius' ship. Its bridge was remarkably similar to the

Cosmos', except that it was decorated with an astrolabe of some kind, and a terrestrial globe.

The Professor engaged the engines and, a few minutes later, we were outside the space-time continuum, slicing our way through the aether towards Earth...

I could tell you more details about Mademoiselle Susanne and how she located Professor Helvetius in Cambridge where he was a don at a local college, but since he expressly asked me to say as little as possible about him, I obviously have no choice but to respect his wishes.

The return journey took place without any untoward incidents. The Professor dropped the five of us back in Normandy, a few yards away from the Doctor's hangar.

Then, his ship rose in the air and disappeared in the direction of the British Channel.

We were greeted by the villagers with cheerful enthusiasm. Now that they knew that the Doctor was a great man of science, nothing seemed to surprise them anymore. Not even the sight of Tiziraou elicited anything more than a few words of pity towards a being whom they took to be an unfortunate freak of nature.

The Doctor expressed some concern about the need for secrecy, and worried about the men blabbing at a local market and word of our extraordinary guest eventually reaching the ears of some official.

I reassured him on that point.

"You have much to learn about French provincial life, Doctor. I grew up in a village much like this one, and I can tell you that you can trust these people to keep your secrets. Yes, they may be an ignorant and superstitious bunch, but they also don't pry into other people's business, and especially, they would never share what they know with foreigners..."

"You mean, the Germans or the British?" asked the old scientist.

"No, I mean any people from anywhere more than 20 miles away, and most of all, Parisians! If anyone from the city inquires about us, he'll get nothing but ambiguous answers. We went away and we came back, that's all they'll find out, if even that. In time, I think you'll learn to appreciate the discretion and hearty common sense of your average Normand. You couldn't have picked a better place to conduct your research..."

I returned to my own cottage where my two servants, Marcel and Pierre, welcomed me back with open arms. After a good dinner, which made me forget all the pills that I had swallowed, I had the unadulterated pleasure of at last sleeping in my own bed for the first time in months... For as I discovered, it was August 4th, 1905, and we had been gone for almost four months...

In the ensuing weeks, I began to write this narrative, and became a regular visitor at the Doctor's workshop... The old scientist had not abandoned his grand project, and had already begun to work on a new *Cosmos*... He was busy designing new parts, and placing orders at Le Creusot...

When I was not assisting the Doctor and Fred, I introduced Tiziraou to life on the planet Earth. With some artificial implements, such as gloves and high-heeled boots, the little Martian could pass for a macrocephalic dwarf of the kind we sometimes see exhibited in freak shows.

Together, we went to Paris, and visited the Museum of Natural History, which greatly interested him. We also went to see *Ariane* at the Opéra, and he took great pleasure in discovering the joys of music, an art which had been completely unknown on Mars.

Sadly, his constitution was soon weakened by Earth's greater gravity and atmosphere, and he began to waste away. We became very concerned about his health, and for a while, I thought he was going to die.

But once again, Doctor Omega came to the rescue and found the right mixture of drugs that enabled Tiziraou to recover.

During his convalescence, I played various melodies on my beloved Stradivarius. I took great pleasure in introducing him to the wonders of Paganini and Vieuxtemps. Tiziraou even began to write a few compositions for me, and I am forced to admit that he showed a great deal of promise. My friend the Duke of Charmerace recently had one performed by the class of Théophile Laforge at the Conservatoire in Paris! I am looking at a copy of the program as I write this...

Next week, I am planning to take Tiziraou to the Paris Observatory. He has studied the most recent maps of Mars, drawn by Schiaparelli and Lowell, and pondered over the ultimate fate of his race... Reminding me that all civilizations, including ours, are indeed mortal...

The Narrative of Denis Borel, January 1906.

It has been two months since I finished my earlier narrative, and I firmly thought that I would not have to take my pen again.

But last night, Doctor Omega came to see me.

His new *Cosmos* is now finished, and he has already planned his next trip with Fred. Over dinner, he told me about it in great detail. Naturally, he wants Tiziraou and I to come along. The little Martian is obviously enthusiastic about the idea, but I confess that I have grave reservations...

Mon Dieu, what to do? What to do?...

Afterword
An Upside Down Doctor

Le Docteur Oméga was first published at the height of the *Belle Epoque* (the French Edwardian era) in a red, cloth-bound hardcover, by *La Librairie Mondiale* of Paris in 1906, with lovely period engravings by E. Bouard and J.-M. Breton.

Its author, Arnould Galopin (1865-1934), was a prolific French writer. Galopin is virtually unknown today; yet, during his life, he won the French Academy Grand Prize for his *Sur le Front de Mer* [*On the Sea Front*] (1918), a critically-acclaimed novel about the Merchant Navy during World War I. The Great War was still eight years in his future when he penned what he undoubtedly intended to be an homage to H. G. Wells' *First Men in the Moon* (1901), complete with a mysterious eccentric scientist, a journey to another world (Mars instead of the Moon, in perhaps another homage to Wells), and a strange space-repelling substance which he initially called *repulsite*, but later changed to *stellite*.

Le Docteur Oméga must have been quite successful for it was almost immediately reissued by pulp publisher

Tallandier as a series of twelve magazines in 1908 under the title *Les Chercheurs d'Inconnu* [*Seekers of the Unknown*]. For that edition, Galopin changed the name of the ship from the *Cosmos* to the *Excelsior*.

Galopin was never a major author nor was he a ground-breaker like Wells or Jules Verne, but he was an old pro who knew how to spin a yarn and follow a trend. He was not unlike a French Edmond Hamilton or a Vargo Statten. His *Le Bacille* (1928), for example, was an uncannily prophetic tale of a mad scientist who uses bacteriological warfare for revenge.

Galopin also penned numerous juvenile novels, such as *Le Tour du Monde de Deux Gosses* [*Two Kids Around The World*] (1908) and *Un Aviateur de 15 Ans* [*A 15-Year Old Aviator*] (1926). He was the author of the detective thriller *L'Homme au Complet Gris* [*The Man In Grey*] (1910), one of the first French Holmesian pastiches, which pits an aging Sherlock Holmes and a young Harry Dickson against Jack the Ripper, and which will be released by Black Coat Press in 2004.

Still, as pointed out by Terrance Dicks, *Doctor Omega* would have remained a mere footnote in the history of French science fiction had it not been for the research we did for *French Science Fiction, Fantasy, Horror and Pulp Fiction*, a mammoth genre encyclopaedia published in 2000 by McFarland, in which we devoted a short section to Galopin (p. 344).

That, in turn, led our friend, British artist Kevin O'Neill, to incorporate two references to *Doctor Omega* in Volume 2 of his and Alan Moore's comic-book series *The League of Extraordinary Gentlemen*, which dealt with a Martian invasion of Earth. One was a shot of Tiziraou himself (Vol. 2, No. 2, illustration at the bottom of page 27), the other, identifying the undersigned as the author of a British Museum report on Doctor Omega (Vol. 2, No. 3, page 14, panel 7).

It is, therefore, fair to say that without Kevin O'Neill, this book would not exist. Afterwards, when solicited to contribute a short story for Abiogenesis Press' magnificent tribute *Alan Moore: Portrait of an Extaordinary Gentlemen* (released in June 2003), it was only natural for us, and French artist Gil Formosa, to create a four-page vignette entitled *An Unearthly Gentleman*, in which we further explored the background of the mysterious Doctor Omega (heretofore left a complete cypher by Arnould Galopin), complete with a reproduction of some of Bouard's original illustrations.

In addition to being struck by the obvious similarities in physical description, temperament, and shall we say, vocational interests, between Doctor Omega and another more famous television Doctor whose granddaughter seemed to know more about French history than her own teacher when we first met her, we also noticed that the Greek letter Omega is also used as an symbol of Ohm, a unit of electrical resistance...

...And we all know what we get when OHM is turned upside down...

Jean-Marc & Randy Lofficier

Printed in the United Kingdom
by Lightning Source UK Ltd.
9670800001B/52-60